Storm Harbor

Tamara Maudelle

Publisher: Tamara Smith

Note to the Reader

Cover Design: JS Designs at jsdesignscoverart.com
Editor: Sarah Lamb at sarahlambwriting.com

ISBN Print: 978-1-7372915-2-7
ISBN EBook: 978-1-7372915-3-4

Printed in the United States of America

 Created with Vellum

To my amazing mother, Collene: God took you to Heaven early last year, but you were always my number one fan and the best mom anyone could ever wish for. I miss you, Mom!

To my sister, Jan, and brother, Rick: for being my Alpha readers and for your continued support and encouragement.

To my friends, Brenda, Wendy, and Marcia: for being my Beta readers. You were constructive and caring and very helpful in assisting me in creating a better novel.

To Chris Cooley, for taking the time to conduct a finally read-through of "Storm Harbor." Your eagle eyes are greatly appreciated.

Chapter One

creech—honk! Blaring car horns pulled me from my hypnotic trance, and I shrieked from the driver's seat. The steering wheel jerked out of my hand by some unseen force, and my vehicle magically returned to the correct lane. My heart raced as I stared in astonishment because not only did I almost kill someone, but somehow, the car corrected my ghastly error all on its own. "What on earth?!" I uttered in amazement and thankfulness. Reaching over, I cranked up the car's air conditioning fan. The frigid cold should help me stay awake, so hopefully, I wouldn't make the dangerous error of falling asleep at the wheel again.

The overwhelming exhaustion could no longer be denied, and I had to get off these roads and rest. Being on the run had taken its toll on my mind and body. My limbs felt sore and numb simultaneously, and fear and anger waged a constant battle within my psyche. Rubbing my aching eyes under the dark sunglasses did little to ease the pain of too little sleep and the blazing glare of the desert sun.

Although it was only around four in the afternoon, I couldn't drive any farther. At least the seemingly endless landscape switched from the arid dry scenery to a lusher vista, but I had to find another small town with an out-of-the-way motel and bed down for the night. Pulling off the side of the road, I placed the old map onto my lap and found what I was looking for. This remote village was perfect, only two more miles down the highway.

As I arrived in town for fuel, I diligently scanned for traffic cams or other surveillance that could spot me or my vehicle. This possible danger kept me vigilant whenever I entered a town, although, luckily, this was a small backwoods community.

Finally, I spotted a self-service station and pulled up to a pump. An elderly gentleman stood by one of the pumps, filling the gas tank of his old, beat-up station wagon, and a young boy played kickball at the side of the station's garage. The ground was barren from lack of rain, and the dust rose as the boy volleyed the ball back and forth between his feet. After getting out of my car, the blast from the summer's heat hit me, and I wiped away the sweat beading my brow. The smell of melting tar, gasoline fumes, and engine oil assaulted my nostrils.

I swiped my untraceable credit card and filled my thirsty gas tank. As I finished the sale, an angry yell sounded from the service bay, and my gaze whipped toward the cacophony.

"Stupid dog! Get the bejesus out of here, you cur!" A young man in oily coveralls and a sweaty red ballcap ran out of the garage chasing a small dark-colored dog; then, he kicked the poor mutt hard in the hip. The pup howled in pain and scuttled into the scrub behind the station. The man shuffled back into the garage, still muttering while wiping his hands on an oil-stained rag.

As I witnessed the assault, a vivid, horrific memory flashed through my mind, and a sharp spasm zigzagged down my chest, settling into my gut. An inner, flaming heat flashed from my core and migrated through my anatomy. I grabbed onto the car's door frame, hoping to stay upright, waiting for the pain and panic to leave my body. My knuckles turned white as I hung on for dear life, and I willed my breathing to return to a normal rhythm. Even my hearing narrowed down to a low whine. Experience taught me how to deal with these panic attacks, and I worked hard to calm everything within me. It took several minutes, but my senses returned to normalcy.

As I started feeling more like myself, I released my fierce grip, flexed my hands to relieve the cramping, and inhaled several more calming breaths. Finally, my shaking fingers locked the car, and I pocketed my keys. Anger filled me because of what that imbecile did to the pup, and I had to do something. Striding purposefully, yet on wobbly legs, I needed to find that abused animal.

The old geezer finally spoke up, shook his head, and warned as I passed, "That kid loves terrorizing that animal and other strays within the town. Don't waste your time, girlie. That hound's been 'round here for months, and he won't let anyone near him. He runs from everybody, and as the day is long, there's no taming that wild thing."

Ignoring the old man, I moved in haste, hoping to find the poor canine. Unfortunately, the little creep kicked that dog hard, and it worried me he could have been seriously injured.

Glancing toward the garage, I muttered, "I'll deal with you later, you little maggot!"

I still couldn't spot the pooch as I moved toward the scrub. Then, looking up ahead, there was a large grove of trees along the back of the gas station's property. I entered the wooded area and whistled for the animal. There was a rustling, then I saw him up ahead, limping badly in his haste to escape. He was good at evading any attempts I made to get closer. I'd go left; he dodged right. When I moved right, he'd hustle back to the left or circle from behind me and run toward the gas station. It was like herding cats, and I was getting nowhere.

"Here, boy. I won't hurt you, baby." As I moved farther into the woods, I kept repeating my words, but I was tiring quickly. The dog proceeded to my left again and wobbled faster in his haste to get away from another human he assumed would abuse him. I tried to keep looking, but after forty minutes, I finally stopped in exhaustion and fell to my knees onto the hard ground.

"Please, baby…I'm only trying to help…." I shifted from kneeling and sat down on my butt. Pulling my knees to my chest and wrapping my arms around them, I gathered what little strength I had left. Pulling oxygen into my lungs, I attempted to call the wounded guy one last time. "Baby, I'm here for you…." I trailed off.

There was nothing left to give. Every molecule of my body refused to cooperate, and I couldn't move or speak another syllable. All I had left were tears. I sobbed, lowering my head to my knees as the pain, anger, fear, and exhaustion spilled down my cheeks. Months of insomnia, constant wariness, anxiety, and having to chase this poor dog left my body and emotions empty. I had no clue how long I'd been crying, but I couldn't stop. The hopelessness filled my soul, and I could no longer hold it at bay.

I heard a noise to my left, but I continued to sob. There was a nudge against my left shoulder, so I peered over my arm to see what had inter-rupted my bout of self-pity. Two big, soulful brown eyes stared back at me. I knew those eyes—they were exactly like the ones that had been staring back at me in the mirror over the past several months. Slowly lifting my head, I eyed the dog I'd been chasing for three-quarters of an hour. He tilted his head, sat down, and rested his chin on my raised knees. I sniffled again, wiped the tears away with my hands, then peered intently at the pup.

Once I lowered my legs, he laid down and gently rested his chin on my thighs. I slowly touched the top of his head and felt his greasy, matted fur. As I continued to run my hand down his body, I encountered more grease and every protruding bone in his emaciated body. This poor thing was in terrible shape. He whimpered, and I realized I'd touched the hip where the jerk kicked him. When he looked at me with such misery, I couldn't help myself and laid down beside him and nestled against his body, ignoring the filth and stench.

I gazed intently into his eyes and said, "I'm so sorry, my friend, I didn't mean to hurt you. What do you say about coming with me? I'll care for you and find you a loving home."

He raised his head, whined again, and licked my cheek.

"I'll take that as a 'yes,' little pup. Let's go." He stood with me, and we slowly strolled back toward the gas station. His awful limp was even more pronounced, but I didn't have the strength to carry him. As we neared the clearing, my new friend paused and looked at me with apprehension.

"Don't worry. That creep won't come near you again. I promise." I made the motion of crossing my heart—he seemed to think about what I'd said, then apparently agreed as we strode back to my car.

After settling him into the back seat, I climbed into the vehicle and drove around to the back of the station, settling for a shady spot under an old tree. I cracked the windows so the dog could get fresh air. After exiting the car, I strode to the trunk.

Looking around, I made sure no one was watching and pulled out a short, dark, spiky brown wig and shoved my long blonde hair inside the wig cap. Next, I grabbed an old, ripped army jacket, a pair of stained painter's pants, and scuffed cowboy boots. After returning to the front seat, I found my makeup kit in my overnight bag and carefully smudged my face with black eyeshadow.

Luckily, the boy playing kickball was nowhere to be seen, and no one else was around. I changed into the clothes from the trunk, slipped on a pair of sunglasses, and waited. From my vantage point, I could see the mechanic's garage as both front and rear doors were wide open. The restrooms were in the back, so I could easily watch if anyone entered or departed the lavatories.

The idiot who kicked the dog had been chugging beer like a dedicated alcoholic, so I knew he'd have to relieve himself soon. All I had to do was bide my time.

I gazed into the rearview mirror and saw the pooch panting in exhaustion and hunger. He was thirsty too. After shoving the plethora of road maps onto the floor, I found my water bottle and an old but clean plastic food container. After filling it with water, I passed it over the seat, and he drank every drop. Opening the cooler in the passenger seat, I discovered remnants from this afternoon's chicken sandwich, shredded the meat and passed that over. It wasn't much, but feeding him a little at a time was safer. The poor guy gulped it down and gave me a silly grin, hoping I'd keep the food coming.

"Sorry, baby. Let that settle first, and I'll gladly give you more." As I turned back around, the moron from the garage was heading to the men's restroom. "I've got to go for a few minutes, so hold the fort, my friend. Don't worry; I'll be back."

I pulled up the collar of my jacket and assured myself that no one else was around to witness me following the man into the restroom. After quietly entering, I jammed the door closed with a stick I'd found outside and tiptoed around a tiled divider wall. Luckily, I spotted the jerk at the

5

urinal, and he was too busy doing his business to notice me. The room smelled of stale urine, and God knows what else. *Yuck!*

He was whistling, which helped to cover the sound of my approach. I waited patiently for him to finish, and as he turned around and zipped up his pants, I kneed him in the groin. He uttered a "whoomph" and fell hard to his knees in pain. I moved behind him and put the creep in a firm yet controlled choke hold. His body stiffened in alarm as he tried to wiggle out of my grasp. It didn't work.

While kneeling beside the abuser, I whispered into his ear, "You like hurting a little dog? That sample I just gave you is how that poor mutt must have felt when you kicked him. He's an innocent creature who deserves your respect, and if I ever hear about you harming another animal, I'll be back, and we'll do this again. You got that?" I still spoke quietly but menacingly.

I released my grip and crept around to face him. The man turned to look at me, but I punched him in the nose, then did a quick kick to his solar plexus. He doubled over and simply laid there, recovering from my assault.

I knelt again and whispered into his ear. "Do you understand me? Will we have to have this dance again?"

He cried and tried to catch his breath, then mumbled, "No...please. I understand." Luckily, he refused to look at me. Satisfaction filled me that I had instilled enough fear in him that maybe, just maybe, he'd never hurt another helpless animal.

"Good. I'm glad we've come to an amicable agreement." I quietly returned to the door, removed the stick, and glanced outside. Then, not seeing any witnesses, I proceeded casually to the car, got in, and slowly drove away. After a few miles, I pulled into a secluded area off the road, removed the wig, wiped my face, and changed my clothes. As I glanced at the dog in the rearview mirror, he looked at me in confusion, tilting his head back and forth.

"Sorry, sweetie. It's only business. Next on our agenda, we need to find a motel and, hopefully, a veterinarian that's still open. You need someone qualified to check you out. Does that sound like a plan?" I turned around, and he replied with a quiet "arf."

It wasn't long before I drove into the town and found the motel. When I went inside to check in, the man at the counter barely looked in my direction, but he glanced outside at my vehicle. He was obese and wore an old, stained, torn, sleeveless t-shirt that revealed massive amounts of body hair. The smell of his sour sweat permeated the small lobby, and I wrinkled my nose at the offensive odor.

"Nice car, lady. What is it, anyway?" He chomped on an old, unlit cigar while he took my cash and wrote me a receipt.

"It's a 1970 Oldsmobile Cutlass 442."

"It's a beauty. Care to sell it?"

"Nah. But thanks for the offer," I answered in a casual yet noncommittal way. "By the way, is there a veterinarian in the area?"

"Yep," was his only reply. To my dismay, the big man coughed up a giant wad of saliva and spewed it into the overflowing and smelly garbage can by the door. *Lovely.*

"Okay...can you give me a phone number or directions, please?" I hoped he'd answer me quickly so I could return outside and breathe in some badly needed fresh air.

He raised his head, looked at me critically, then peered at my car. "Lady, if you got an animal, it'll cost you another fifty bucks for the room. They can do a lot of damage."

"That's not a problem. Here's another fifty." I handed him the money, and he looked at the car again, trying to see what was behind the darkly tinted windows. My fingers tapped impatiently against the worn and scarred Formica of the reception countertop.

"It's only one small dog. He's harmless." I cringed on the inside because I couldn't verify my statement. I'd only known the dog for less than an hour.

The hefty man behind the counter chewed again on his unlit cigar, sized me up once more, then gave me the phone number and address of the veterinarian.

"Thanks." I grabbed the room key, and as I was about to leave, a short, skinny elderly gentleman shuffled into the lobby. He flashed me a grin and a quick greeting.

When the old man glanced at the guy behind the counter, his grin turned to a grimace. "Dang it, Gomer! What did I tell you about taking your shower? This place reeks of you, son! Get out of here and clean up—and on your way out, dump that filthy garbage."

Gomer's face turned into a pout, and he muttered, "Sorry, pop." The big, smelly, hairy man stood up and did as he was told. As he walked by his father, the older gentleman kindly patted his son on the back, at least as far as he could reach on the big guy, and told him he loved him.

As I returned to my vehicle, I couldn't help but smile at the bizarre relationship between the two men. I admired the old man for disciplining his son while reminding his kid he still loved him. This dynamic was unfamiliar to me, but I found it somewhat comforting. *Hmm.*

After the dog greeted me, I settled behind the wheel, pulled out one of my disposable cell phones, and dialed the vet's number. It rang several times before someone in a breathless voice answered.

"Anderson Animal Clinic."

"Hello. I have a stray dog that needs immediate attention. I know it's late, but could I bring him in now?"

"I just closed the clinic, but you say he's injured?"

I gave the vet as much information as I knew about the dog, which wasn't much, and she agreed to see him.

After arriving at the clinic, I coaxed the poor mutt into the building, and the female vet was waiting behind the reception counter. The place smelled clean, and I smiled at the numerous animal photos on the walls.

"Oh my," she said. She walked over and knelt next to the dog. The mutt growled and bared ferocious teeth. I shushed the dog in a no-nonsense tone, and he sat back on his haunches and smiled widely. This surprised the veterinarian, and me as well.

"What's his name?"

"I don't know…I hadn't thought about it." But then, I remembered I met the little dog in Boone County. "Hmm. Boone…his name is Boone."

"Boone it is. Come on back, and let's have a look at him." The vet allowed the dog to sniff her hand, and she gently touched the top of his head. He cooperated and let her pet him. After a moment, she stood and reached over to me with her right hand. "I'm Dr. Cheryl Anderson."

Shaking her hand in appreciation, I stuttered in response, "I'm S… Hannah Renault." I could have kicked myself for almost saying the wrong name. *Come on, Hannah. Giving your real name could get you killed.*

Dr. Anderson stared at me for a brief second but then ushered us into an exam room. After she checked Boone's vitals, she palpitated his hip, drew some blood, and replied she'd take him for an x-ray. She returned several minutes later and said his hip was fine, only severely bruised.

"Other than the bad contusion and being severely underweight, he's in good shape. I'll send you home with pain meds, liquid vitamins, and a supply of dog food—including how to feed and care for an emaciated dog. Also, I'd recommend you get him neutered and vaccinated as soon as he's recovered and put on adequate weight. I'm estimating his age is around five, but there's no way to know for sure."

I nodded and thanked her for the help. As I was about to pick up the dog, she halted my movements and said, "How about we give him a bath before you go?"

"Thank heavens! He reeks, and I'd love to get him smelling like a rose." I smiled widely in appreciation as I carried him to the washing area in another room. It took three baths to get down to the dog's natural, and surprisingly, mostly white coat. He had brown ears with brown spots on his head, face, and belly, and a large one on his lower back.

"Well, look at that, Boone! You're positively handsome. You don't even have fleas and ticks, but I suppose all the grease kept them at bay," Dr. Anderson praised. Boone grinned with pleasure and licked her cheek. She laughed happily and kissed the top of Boone's head. He answered with a happy "arf" and gave us a silly smile.

"I don't know how to thank you for helping Boone and me. I'm only in town for the night, so you taking him quickly was a blessing."

After paying her, I shook her hand, and before we walked out the door, she said, "I won't have the heartworm test results back until morning. Can you call me around eight?"

"That would be great," I replied. Dr. Anderson helped me take the meds and food to my car, and she lifted Boone into the backseat. He was drowsy from the pain medicine, and his stomach seemed happier now that he had eaten more food at the vet's office.

Waving goodbye, I stopped at a store to pick up a few supplies, then

Boone and I headed back to the motel. I lugged my bags into the room, and Boone followed me diligently inside. Finally, he was happy and ready for a comfortable place to sleep.

To my pleasant surprise, the room was clean and smelled of flowers. "Well, Boone, after the horrific stench of the motel lobby, I was afraid our room would be a garbage pit. Thank goodness it's spic and span, my boy!"

That night, I ate the food from the store deli, then fed and watered Boone using the new bowls I'd purchased. It surprised me later when he went to the door and wanted outside to relieve himself. *Had he belonged to someone in his early years and had some training?*

At the store, I'd also picked up some toys for Boone and a padded dog bed. I set the puppy mattress on the floor at my bedside. He sniffed, shoved it around with his nose, and finally climbed in and snuggled down.

As soon as I crawled under my covers, the pup whined and barked until I lifted him onto the mattress beside me; so much for the dog bed.

"All right, Boone, but no snoring because I need a good night's sleep." He grinned his cute doggy smile and settled close to my side. I quickly fell asleep, but the dreaded nightmares returned.

"You stupid, ugly imbecile! Why do you make me do this? You know how I want my veal prepared, so why can't you be a good little wifey and do it correctly? I own this town and everyone in it, and you know I own you as well, so do as you're told. Then I wouldn't have to punish you." I wait in terror for another punch, kick, or slap. Sometimes it's all three. He calls me crude, insulting names, slaps me hard in the face, and punches me in the stomach. I fly back against the kitchen counter, then onto the tiled floor. Trying hard to catch my breath, I struggle to breathe any air that will keep me alive.

"I told you this would happen. It just proves how stupid and useless you are, and I don't know why I put up with your crap. You can't do anything right!"

My husband of two years pulls me up from the floor by grabbing my throat and shakes me until my teeth rattle. He then turns me around and tosses me across the expensive marble island, and I hit the cold, hard floor, my hip taking the brunt of the fall. Storming over, he stands glaring at me with fisted hands, and I curl myself into a ball and wait for another blow. I hear him breathing hard as if he's been running a marathon. Staying in a fetal position, I wonder which part of my anatomy he'll attack next. After a few moments, I feel a hard kick in my ribs, and he spits into my hair and storms from the room. He slams the front door, and I hear the roar as he starts the engine of his Ferrari and screeches down the circle driveway.

After several minutes, I move cautiously, straightening my body and ensuring everything still works. It hurts to breathe, so I expect he's either bruised or broken more of my ribs. They'd just healed from the last time he kicked me in one of his rages. I struggle to my feet and hang on tightly to the edge of the counter, waiting for the dizziness to pass. Then, moving slowly to the half bath off the kitchen, I shuffle to the mirror. A huge wad of spittle is stuck in my long, dark brown hair, and my face is already swelling and red. Lifting my shirt, my stomach, ribs, and hip are already purple. He's usually careful not to leave visible bruises or cuts, so he aims to punish the trunk of my body or anywhere that can be hidden by clothing.

Grabbing a washcloth, I clean the saliva out of my hair. I stumble back into the kitchen and head for the freezer, grabbing a few dishtowels on the way. Filling the towels with ice, I move slowly to the living room and place the ice packs on my injuries. As I sit gently on the ornate sofa, I feel one of my ribs move, and an intense pain overcomes me, and I'm struggling to breathe again. Unfortunately, I realize it's back to the E.R. It's a long drive to the clinic in Marlowe, but it's where he insists I go if I'm too cowardly to take the pain of his deserving punishments. I slowly move off the sofa, grab my purse and keys, and shuffle to the Mercedes in the garage.

My nightmare moves to one night in our bedroom. He's impotent again and takes out his frustration on me. Ripping my nightgown off, he throws me against the dresser. "It's all your fault! You're so ugly and stupid that I can't have sex with you. You're pitiful and sexless; no man will ever want you!" I run out of the bedroom, but he catches me at the top of the stairs. I trip and start tumbling down the endless descent of steps. I feel the jarring impact of the hardwood treads on every inch of my body. The pain is excruciating.

. . .

I JERKED AWAKE AND STIFLED A SCREAM. SHAKING MY HEAD, I STRUGGLED to find the lamp where it should have been, and remembered I was in the motel room. Spotting it on the other side of the bed, I turned on the light and felt the weight of Boone as he moved over to lay on top of me. The poor thing whined and shook with fear. His soulful eyes stared into my face, and I pulled him close and hugged him, trying to gain a sense of sanity. We both trembled, and I gently crooned to him, trying to calm his anxiety and my own.

"It's alright, baby. We're both okay, and it was only a bad dream. I'm okay; I'm okay, I'm okay…." I kept repeating the mantra until I believed it. My nightgown was soaking wet, and I was chilled to the bone. When we both stopped shuddering, I climbed out of bed, grabbed a clean gown and underwear, and went into the bathroom. Boone stayed close to my heels and refused to leave my side. I opted for another hot shower and a tall glass of cold water and returned to bed. Boone settled back down but continued to snuggle close. I was thankful for the love of this precious guy. Leaving the lamp on, I maneuvered my body around my new, devoted friend.

As I stared across the room at the faded wallpaper wishing for sleep, I knew it was only a matter of time before the violence caught up with me again—and this time, it could take my life.

Chapter Two

The following day, I called Dr. Anderson, and she said, "Boone is heartworm free, and his other tests are fine too. But, of course, he needs plenty of good food. But Hannah, when you reach your final destination, see to it that he's neutered, vaccinated, and receives heartworm prevention."

"Thanks! You've been very kind, and I'll follow your recommendations."

After ending the call, I fed Boone, packed up my few belongings, and grabbed the things I'd purchased for the dog. He followed me to the car, except for a quick jaunt to the grass to relieve himself, then we climbed in.

Boone insisted on sitting in the front passenger seat, and I didn't argue. I was happy for his close company. But, unfortunately, I realized I'd forgotten something as I was about to pull out of the parking lot.

"Crap!" I muttered under my breath. Then, putting the car back into park, I reached above me to the visor and pulled out a small slip of paper. Boone eyed me with puzzlement.

"Sorry, bub. I promised someone's grandson, and I have to honor it. It'll only take a minute."

After I opened the slip of paper, I recited the words, "St. Michael the

Archangel, defend us in battle, be our protection against the wickedness and snares of the devil. May God rebuke him, we humbly pray, and do thou, O Prince of the heavenly host, by the divine power of God, cast into Hell, Satan and all the evil spirits who prowl around the world seeking the ruin of souls. Amen."

As I said the prayer, Boone tilted his head back and forth, wondering what I was trying to tell him.

"I know. I don't believe in God but vowed to honor a good person's request. The man who kindly gave me this vehicle for free only had one condition: I promise to say this prayer once a day before I drive the Cutlass. I told him reciting it doesn't mean anything to me, but he insisted, and I agreed—I don't break promises, my friend.

"Now, I need to pick up a quick breakfast, and we'll head back to the highway."

We did just that, and I bought Boone some scrambled eggs. I fed him slowly, and he gratefully accepted and gulped every bite. When he finished eating, I pulled the maps off the floor and found the one for Kansas.

"I'm hoping we'll reach the outskirts of Topeka by nightfall. Then tomorrow morning, it should be safe to travel the major highways."

After I gave him a couple of dog toys, Boone settled down into the seat. I donned a pair of sunglasses, stuffed a wad of bubblegum into my mouth, and pulled onto a less-traveled paved road. There weren't any cameras on these highways, so I should be safe from prying eyes.

It turned out the dog was great company. He enjoyed the rock and roll music blaring from the stereo and even howled a few times when I sang too loudly.

I stopped at an isolated diner for lunch and picked up better-quality food: baked chicken, broccoli, and carrots. I even ordered the same thing for Boone.

Parking the car in a shady spot behind a small grocery store, I took Boone out of the car on a collar and leash. I let him take care of business, then we both enjoyed our lunch together under a large maple tree. When we were done, I put the dog back in the car, lowered the windows, and ran into the store to grab a bottled water, granola bars, chocolate, and some fresh fruit. Boone was thrilled I'd returned and licked my face earnestly when I climbed into the driver's seat.

"I'm fine, bub. I told you I always keep my promises, so you know I'd never abandon you." I kissed the top of his bony head and drove back onto the highway.

After about an hour, I smelled something atrocious in the car.

"What in tarnation is that horrific stench?" I glanced at Boone, and he made his usual laughing face; then I heard a loud toot coming from his behind. He wouldn't look at me as he let out another smelly, noisy fart.

I couldn't help myself and covered my nose with my hand and quickly cranked down the driver's window. "Boone, that's so bad! Okay, pal, we'll find a place to pull over—and quickly too!"

Finding a dirt side road, I pulled off by a grove of trees. Grabbing the cooler from the back seat and the dog bowl, we headed to the woods. Boone took off toward a large grassy area. He circled several times, then moved to another location and spun again. Boone did this two more times and it worried me.

"Boone, come on, boy. You need to do your business." After a few minutes, he finally found the right spot and dumped a large pile. It was loaded with bright green broccoli.

I couldn't help myself and giggled, attempting to hide my laughter by turning away. When I glanced back at him, he squatted again. When the poor dog returned my gaze, he pulled his ears close to his head in grief.

"I'm sorry, sweetie. I have the feeling your body doesn't like broccoli, so I promise to remember that in the future. We'd better stick with the food from the vet until you're healthy again—and definitely no more broccoli." He grinned sheepishly and moved to another spot to drop another steaming pile.

I decided we'd better stay in the woods for a little while until I was sure he'd finished. In the meantime, I found the bottle of the pink stuff in my supplies, and before he knew what I was doing, I shoved a spoonful into his mouth and down his throat. He made a gagging sound and gave me a dirty look.

"Trust me, baby; it'll help. The vet said this stuff is safe for you and will make you feel better. I hope you'll forgive me, my friend."

I sat on the ground and leaned back against an old oak tree. Grabbing a bottle of water and his bowl from the cooler, I gave him a cool drink. He lapped it up and sat beside me, cradling his head in my lap. Boone fell into a deep sleep.

As I sat there, my mind drifted back to the last time I'd fallen down the long staircase at the house.

As I lay unmoving on the floor, I hear him come down the steps, and he stands before me. I remember staring at his twelve-hundred-dollar shoes, wondering if he'll kick me with his expensive loafers. But instead, I hear him swear as he taps his foot. I watch the tassels of his shoe bounce up and down with the rhythm of the steady beat.

"Now look what you've done. You're utterly useless, and I'll have to take time out of my busy schedule to take you to a doctor because of your clumsiness."

I move slowly to check my limbs, but when I try to raise my left arm, there's a sharp, intense pain in my collarbone. My ribs also hurt when I inhale. Sitting up slowly, I pretend there's nothing amiss.

"I'm fine. You go ahead to your golf game."

"I should think so. If you decide to see the doc, you know where you have to go and what to say. Right, stupid?" I nod my head in submission. "Good. Make sure you clean yourself up because you look like a starving, ragged waif from Kirby Street. It's disgusting."

Kirby Street is an area in the unseemly part of town where he loves to drive around in his fancy car and ridicule and mimic the poor homeless people. He always keeps the darkly tinted windows up so none of the people on the street hear his blatant insults.

I focus on his shoes and dare not raise my gaze. It only angers him further if I lock my eyes with his when he's in one of his moods.

I hear the door slam, his car start up, and I wait until I can no longer hear the engine's rumble.

Testing my legs, I slowly and gingerly stand and shuffle to the hall mirror. Pulling my silk blouse from my shoulder, I see an angry bump along my collarbone, and moving my arm is impossible. I wonder if my shoulder is dislocated as well.

After straightening my clothes and finding my lost shoes from the tumble down the stairs, I grab my purse and slowly amble to my car. Getting in isn't easy, but I make it and have to drive using only my right arm. I know the trip will take about two hours to the small town my husband insists I go to when I have my "accidents." As usual, I'll have to use a fake name at the clinic, but they know me well.

When I arrive, I shuffle over to the receptionist, and she smiles kindly and hands me paperwork on a clipboard. After several minutes, the doctor I know by name comes out to greet me. Her smile is cautious and knowing. She helps me stand, walks me to an exam room, and guides me to sit on the table.

"What is it this time, honey? Did you trip again?" she asks with kindness.

"Yes. You know me—I'm so clumsy, Annie."

"Mm-hmm. Let's get you into a gown, and then I can take a look at you."

After she examines me, she clucks her tongue a few times, then finally says, "Your collarbone is likely broken, so you'll need an x-ray. Your shoulder is fine. The pain from the fracture in your collarbone is causing the pain in your arm. You'll be black and blue all over for a while, though."

After an x-ray, she advises me my collarbone is broken, and her recommendations are a sling and pain meds. After I dress, she helps me into the sling, then gives me some over-the-counter pain medication. I'm about to get off the table, but she raises her hand to stop me from leaving.

"Serena, I know who you are and what's happening." I'm about to deny it, but she stops me and says, "You're Serena St. John, married to Trace St. John. Trace and his family own the town of Scribner and pretty much everyone in it and have for years."

I say nothing, and she continues, "He's beating the crap out of you, and you're going to have to leave him before he kills you." I keep my eyes downcast and remain quiet.

"Serena, I know this because I was once like you. I wasn't married to a rich man from an influential family, but he was just as vicious and cruel. We were together for four years, and I simply took the abuse. But then I realized I was pregnant and knew I had to get out—I had to protect the baby."

Raising my gaze to look at her, I see the truth and pain in her expression. She lays her hand over mine and gives me a kind smile.

"How long has he been beating you, Serena?"

I don't respond for a moment, then quietly say, "It's going on two years now."

"You have to leave him."

"I can't. As you know, his family owns the town and everyone in it—the judge, the police, the lawyers, the doctors...it's impossible. I've been racking my brain trying to figure out how to get out, but I can't find a solution. He controls everything in my life—including the money. I get nothing, and he does it deliberately." I feel a tear of anger slide down my cheek and brush it away in frustration.

"What about your family? Can they help?"

"I have no family...there's no one." My phone vibrates, and I know it's him texting me. As I gaze at the screen, he's asking where I am and to get home where I belong. Annie sees the message and nods knowingly.

"Control. He loves it, doesn't he?"

I nod my head in response.

"Serena, I can help you, but it won't be easy. Nothing of value is. But once you decide to do this, there's no turning back. You understand?"

I raise my eyes back to hers. "Yes. I want out." My tone is firm with conviction.

"Here's my number. Is there any way you can call me from another phone? Like a payphone from a grocery store, gas station—one he can't trace?"

"Yes. There's a gas station just outside of Scribner. He makes me volunteer at the homeless shelter next door because it makes him look good in the papers. Trace detests the homeless, but my volunteering makes him look like a saint. I'm supposed to go there tomorrow afternoon at two."

"Call me. I'll answer it, and we'll begin planning. Just act normal and do anything you must to stay out of his way."

My phone vibrates again, and I have to answer. I quickly tell him that I'll be home in two hours after leaving the clinic. Annie nods at me, squeezes my hand again, and I leave the building, clutching the card with her phone number as if my life depends on it. And it does.

Chapter Three

My mind returned to the present, and thirty minutes had passed. Boone felt me stir, and when he woke up, he looked at me with his goofy smile.

"You're feeling better?"

"Arf!"

We got up and strolled around the wooded area, giving him time to stretch his legs. It also gave him another chance to rid himself of any remaining broccoli. Luckily, his stomach recovered, and we returned to the car.

The rest of the trip to Topeka remained uneventful. We checked in when I found another non-descript town with a cheap yet clean motel. This time, a kind, gray-haired older woman named Hazel greeted us from behind the counter. She even insisted on meeting Boone. So I brought him into the office, and he was a perfect gentleman. He even licked Hazel's cheek, and she laughed with delight.

After the introductions, she said, "He's awfully skinny, dear."

"I know. We just met a couple of days ago, and I'm seeing that he eats well and puts on weight. He's already seen a vet, and she gave him a clean bill of health—except for the skin and bones issue."

"You're a good young woman, hun. But, while you're in town, just be careful. This isn't the best area crime-wise, so make sure you take care of yourself, including the pup."

"Thanks. I'll do that. Can you recommend a restaurant that offers decent takeout?"

"Sure. O'Casey's has great food, and they're reasonable. Just go left out of the parking lot, and they're located a block down the road on your right. By the way, I'd love to watch your baby if you'd like to have a sit-down and leisurely dinner at the restaurant."

"Really? That'd be great, thanks!" I kneeled next to Boone and cradled his face in my hands. "How'd you like to stay with Hazel while I have dinner, bub?"

Boone grinned with happiness and wagged his tail. "Arf!"

"I believe that's a yes, Hazel. He's all yours."

"Take your time, dear." I thanked her and left her a can of dog food and instructions on feeding Boone.

It was a hot and humid summer evening, and the restaurant was packed. Luckily, I found a parking space at the rear of the establishment under a security light.

The dinner was delicious, and it was just what I needed. I even treated myself to a glass of wine to wash down the meal. It was after nine by the time I finished the four-course dinner.

After digging out my car keys, I exited the restaurant's rear door and strolled toward the Oldsmobile. But as I walked around several cars and spotted mine, I saw a commotion and jumped behind a large blue truck.

Three teenage boys walked around my car—admiring the rebuilt and souped-up Cutlass. I heard them whistle, and one of them said, "This baby is just waiting for me to take it home. Ain't you, beautiful?" He whistled again as he ran his hand across the hood. His friends hooted in agreement.

"Come on, Rocky, let's take it!"

The boy called Rocky pulled out a long piece of metal, which I knew was called a slim jim, and he was about to insert it into the car's window between the window and the door's edge to unlock it. But when the three boys huddled around each other to cover Rocky's crime, their pants were swiftly pulled down to their ankles.

"What the...." Rocky screeched. They looked around, trying to figure out what had happened. The delinquents pulled their pants back up, and Rocky attempted to insert the piece of metal into the edge of the window again. But this time, Rocky was picked up by some unseen force and tossed into the bed of an old rusty pickup that was parked next to my vehicle. The two other boys stared in shock and didn't know what to do.

Rocky sat up, peered over the truck bed, and angrily yelled, "Which of you did that?"

The smaller boy said, "It wasn't us—honest."

Rocky climbed back out of the truck and slowly approached my car. "One of you unlock the door."

The two boys left standing by the Cutlass glanced at each other, shrugged their shoulders, and the shorter boy picked up the metal tool. He inserted it but was also picked up and thrown into the same bed of the old truck. I heard his scream during his entire unexpected flight.

"Come on. This is stupid, man! Someone's playing a trick on us," Rocky said, yet I could hear his voice shaking in fear.

The three boys slowly and cautiously returned to the Oldsmobile's driver door. This time when they touched the vehicle, every stitch of clothing was torn from their bodies. Their attire had vanished into thin air. They screamed in alarm and tried desperately to cover their private parts.

Several people had exited the restaurant by this time and witnessed the three boys naked as jaybirds. The mischievous lawbreakers ran away while they attempted to cover their nakedness. The boys shrieked in terror as they escaped behind another building.

Everyone laughed with glee, including me. One man among the diners said, "Rocky and those boys never learn. They're lousy criminals." His companions all agreed while they strolled to their vehicles, still snickering as they went.

I walked over to my car and spied the slim jim lying on the ground by the door. Kicking it away, I cautiously neared the driver's door. Standing there, I feared touching the car I'd been driving for several days, wondering if I'd be attacked by whatever went after the boys. Reaching out carefully, I touched the window with the tip of my index finger, which I quickly withdrew, then wrapped my arms around myself, protecting my clothing. Nothing happened. I took out my key and shakily inserted it into the lock. So far, so good. Opening the door, I poked my head into the car, looked around, and everything appeared normal. Backing my head out, I carefully raised my foot to step in, then quickly pulled it out again. I cautiously glanced left and right, up and down, as if I'd be attacked by the unseen force. But, again, all was quiet.

Gazing around the outside of the vehicle, I finally released the big gush of air I'd been holding and said, "This is stupid! Just get into the car, scaredy-cat." I quickly climbed in and sighed in relief. My hands still shook, and I felt like an idiot. Then, something fell out of the visor, and I screamed like a two-year-old. Once the shock passed, I picked up the paper. It was the St. Michael prayer.

"Nah—can't be. That's ridiculous. It's only a prayer, and He doesn't exist, right?" I muttered the question to myself in denial. The car's horn gave a brief, loud honk, and there was silence again. My eyes grew wide and I sat there, contemplating the events of the last several minutes.

"You don't say," was all I could utter.

THE NEXT DAY WE MADE IT OUT OF KANSAS AND THROUGH MISSOURI, THEN just inside the border of Illinois. Exhaustion filled me by the time I stopped, and I searched desperately for a decent motel. As I drove past one then another, Boone barked loudly at a specific inn that was decidedly too seedy.

"Are you sure, Boone? It looks pretty bad to me."

"Arf, arf!" He was determined I should stop at this one, and he paced in circles in the passenger seat.

"Okay, okay. Smogger's Motel it is."

I pulled in and drove up to the entrance. The establishment was in terrible shape, and I was concerned this wasn't a good idea. Muttering under my breath that I was an idiot for listening to a dog's opinion, I exited the car.

Upon entering the tiny lobby, a grizzled old man sat at the counter, and he offered me a broad and friendly smile. He wore a bright Hawaiian shirt and clean blue jeans, and his braided gray beard was the longest I'd ever seen. "Welcome, my dear. I assume you'd like a room? Our home may look mangy on the outside, but our rooms are clean, neat, and blessed by the Lord."

Raising my eyebrow in skepticism, I politely answered that I needed a room. I also advised him I had a small, well-behaved dog with me.

"That's wonderful, child. All of God's creatures are welcome. If you'd fill this out, please, we take cash or credit. Whichever you prefer."

"Cash will work. Thank you."

After paying the nice man, I went to the car and drove around back. After leaving the vehicle, Boone took a moment to relieve himself in the grass, and we entered the room. Several crucifixes, religious statues, and framed prayers covered the walls. Even the bedspread was adorned with scripture.

"This is beyond overdone. I bet the Sistine Chapel doesn't display so many religious icons. At least this place is clean. Come on, my friend; you need to be fed. I can only manage a couple of granola bars for myself. I'm beat."

After we ate, I took a long hot shower and donned my nightshirt and a pair of fuzzy socks. Boone snuggled next to me on the bed, and I flipped on the television. I found a national news station. It wasn't long before the news item I'd been dreading appeared in full color.

"Now from Nevada, the powerful businessman Trace St. John and his wife Serena are still missing. Their disappearance has puzzled the family as well as local authorities. Trace's younger brother Cameron is asking for your help in finding his beloved brother and sister-in-law."

I rolled my eyes and mumbled in disgust, "Right...his beloved brother. Their jealousy of each other surpasses the angst between Cain and Abel."

Cameron appeared on the screen and spoke into several microphones. Alligator tears were in his eyes as he looked into the camera, "My dear brother and his wife have been missing for several days, and if someone has any verifiable information regarding their disappearance, my family and I are offering a one-hundred-thousand-dollar reward. Thank you." The news station showed a photo of Trace. Thank goodness they didn't broadcast any pictures of me. But then, Trace rarely permitted them because I was usually sporting some bruise or cut that couldn't be covered by makeup, no matter how hard I tried.

I turned off the screen and snuggled down under the covers. Boone dug at the blanket and insisted on sleeping nestled against my side. He licked my cheek, and I kissed his nose.

"I love you too, my sweet boy."

THE AWFUL DREAM RETURNS. I'M TEN YEARS OLD, AND MY STEPFATHER, HANK, *attempts to touch me in my private place again. I moan in terror in my sleep and unconsciously curl my body into a fetal position under the blankets.*

"You know you like it, Seesee." I hate his nickname for me, and just hearing it makes me want to vomit.

"Nooo. Stop it!" I yell in distress and try to pull his hand away. "I'll tell Mommy!"

"No, you won't. She thinks you're tempting me with your evil ways and are such a bad little girl. Your mommy said that Jesus hates you for what you make me do to you. Now just lay back and enjoy it." He leans down to me and thrusts his tongue into my mouth. I bite down hard, and he pulls back in anger and slaps my face with such force my ears are ringing. "You little whore! I'll make you pay."

He starts unbuckling his pants, and I shrink back in terror. I know it's only a matter of time before he rapes me—and it looks like it will happen tonight. He's naked from the waist down, and I stare in horror at his groin. The stench of his sweat, bad breath, and cigarette smoke assaults my nostrils. As he moves closer, there's a loud banging on the front door. Hank swears loudly and tries to continue his heinous activities, but the knocking persists. He curses once more, gets up, and pulls on his pants.

"I'll be back and we'll finish this, you little demon." His violent words cause saliva to run down his chin, and he turns and storms out the door.

I jump out of bed, get dressed, put on my coat, stuff my backpack with whatever I can grab, and climb out the window. "I'm never coming back. Never!"

. . .

I SAT UP IN BED, FILLED WITH TERROR. AFTER A FEW MOMENTS, I TRIED TO stem the sobs racking my body. Boone licked the tears from my face as he whined and tried to snuggle tightly against me. I buried my head in his neck and breathed in his clean scent. He continued to whimper softly yet rubbed his head back and forth against my face. Gathering him close, I kissed him and let his calming presence soothe my soul.

"Thank you, my precious Boone. You're such a wonderful and loyal friend." I sniffed and grabbed a few tissues to blow my nose and wipe my eyes. After climbing out of bed, I shuffled to the bathroom, turned on the light, and splashed cool water on my face. As I stared at myself in the mirror, the old hurt and haunted gaze from my childhood reflected back at me. Peering closer, all I could see were my dark brown, slightly upward-slanted eyes that were still shadowed by my childhood trauma. Even thinking about it sent terror through me. As usual, I shoved the feelings to the back of my mind and tried to focus on the here and now.

Boone rubbed against my leg, gave one tender little bark, and grinned widely as he smirked at me.

"You seem to know, don't you, boy?"

"Arf!" It was a quiet answer, but I knew he understood my feelings. So I picked him up, kissed him again, and returned to bed. Boone fell asleep, but I laid there, worrying about what could be headed my way. And I knew it wasn't good.

Chapter Four

The next morning, I diligently said the prayer after Boone and I climbed into the car. According to my estimation, it should take us approximately two more days to reach the outskirts of Storm Harbor, Michigan. I stared at the sheet of paper for a moment, shook my head, and tucked it carefully under the visor. Taking advantage of a fast-food restaurant, I purchased a breakfast sandwich and a large black coffee, then returned to the highway.

Boone ogled my sandwich with anticipation, and I returned his compassionate gaze. "Sorry, babe, you had your breakfast, and until your body is up-to-snuff, my food is off limits." He pinned his ears to his head in resignation, so I kissed him, and his goofy grin reappeared.

As I turned around a corner heading out of town, I saw an older Asian gentleman riding a bicycle. I carefully gave him plenty of room with my vehicle, and he waved in thanks and greeting. Seeing this man brought back a vivid memory of the person who saved my life.

THAT NEXT DAY AFTER SEEING THE DOCTOR AT THE OUT-OF-TOWN CLINIC, I'M able to call her, and she provides a name and phone number of a man named Kogi. She pronounces his name Kojee, and I ask her what he can do for me and my situation.

"My dear, trust me. Kogi saved my life, and he'll do the same for you. Call him right away. Time's a-wastin'. You can call me again if you need anything, but Kogi will take good care of you. May God bless you, Serena."

"God has nothing to do with it, Annie. He doesn't exist, and I don't believe in Him," I say disgustingly.

"Oh, love, sure he does. And trust me, He believes in you."

I quietly snort in denial but thank her kindly and disconnect the call. Standing there for several minutes, I debated whether to contact this man. But something inside eggs me on, and I dial the number. A deep voice with a strong Asian accent answers.

"Kogi here. What can I do for you? Need lessons? I instruct in Judo, Karate, Taekwondo, and many more. What is your pleasure?"

I pause, then finally reply, "Annie gave me your number."

He didn't respond right away. Was he going to hang up on me? "I see," he finally answers. "She told me about you and that you may be calling. So you're the broken collarbone lady?" His heavy Asian accent has vanished, and he speaks clear American.

"Uh...yes."

"She told me your husband has you volunteering at the homeless shelter. I have a small studio above the shelter that isn't advertised, so no one will know. When will you be volunteering at the shelter again?"

"Thursday."

"Good. Come up the stairs and knock twice, then three times. Then, I'll know it's you. I trust that you'll show up. If you want to live in freedom and away from the jerk, I'll see you there."

FROM THAT THURSDAY FIVE MONTHS AGO UNTIL I LEFT THAT HORRIBLE town, Kogi trained me in street-smart self-defense. He saved my life. I loved that man with my whole being and would be forever grateful to him. It was hard work and in the beginning, we had to be careful with my broken collar bone. But after several lessons, I knew I could take care of myself, and he also gave me tips on how to stay out of the way of Trace's fists and feet.

I thought again about how the plan was put into place for me to leave Trace, and I remembered it vividly.

ONE DAY, WHEN I WALK IN FOR MY FINAL LESSON, KOGI SEES MY BLACK EYE *and bloody lip. He hangs his head in sorrow, then gives me a fatherly hug. He has me follow him to his office when we finish the class.*

After we sit down, he says, "Your training is complete, and you know it's time for you to run. As we discussed previously, I have what you'll need to start a new life. Your new name will be Hannah Renault, and this envelope contains your new driver's license, an untraceable credit card, and some cash that should tide you over for a while. I'll also include an unregistered and secure phone for us to communicate. However, I'll still advise you use it only when necessary.

"Once you're on the road, I recommend you buy some disposable phones—they're your safest bet for general use. There are also keys to a vehicle my grandson has kindly donated, along with proof of insurance, title, and registration. He's talented at rebuilding cars, and this one he specialized just for you. Don't worry—it's all under your new name.

"When you decide exactly when you'll leave your husband, use the phone I've given you and text this number. My grandson will send you an address where he'll meet you. He will then review the vehicle with you, as well as the enhancements he's made to the car for your protection. In the car's trunk will be a suitcase with suitable clothing for you as well as wigs and a plethora of anything else you may require.

"You'll also need to know we'll be acquiring a body of a young woman with your likeness to use when we trash your vehicle. We want to make sure your husband and the authorities think you're dead," Kogi says with no emotion.

"Wait—what?! I never agreed to killing someone!" I pace the room, and panic sets in.

"Serena—that's not what I said. My grandson is in medical school, and one of the bodies stored in their anatomy lab will fit the bill. He already

checked, and he's doing his best to keep the corpse to the back of the line for class." Kogi stares at me intently until I understand. I nod my head, but I'm thunderstruck by this information.

Kogi continues, "When traveling, stay off any main roads with cameras —especially at the beginning of your road trip. Select out-of-way motels, stores, gas stations, etc., and remain cognizant of any surveillance there as well. Once you reach your final destination, please text me to let me know you've made it.

"One more thing. Something strange happened a week ago that I find odd, yet a blessing. An attorney named Stanley Merrick from Storm Harbor, Michigan, contacted me. A certified letter from his office arrived, informing me that Hannah Renault was the beneficiary of a cottage in Storm Harbor. It's located on Lake Huron in the thumb of Michigan. Be that as it may—I was listed as the go-between, so to speak, and was appointed to handle all communication regarding said inheritance until you arrive in Storm Harbor. What's so strange about this is that we hadn't yet assigned you a new name. So how has this home been left to you under your new identity by this unknown person? After many conversations with this attorney, as well as in-depth investigations, we verified this man and the inheritance are legit. Your new I.D., social security number, and fake address all match up. It's a real conundrum but a wonderful blessing." Kogi scratches his head but smiles in satisfaction.

"You've got to be kidding. Are you sure about all this? Have I inherited a home? But I don't have any family, so it doesn't make sense," I reply with confusion.

"Yup. Now you have a home to call your own, and a safe one at that. Just do everything I've instructed, and you'll be fine. We also have your exit strategy in place, so you pick the date and time. Godspeed, my child."

THINKING ABOUT KOGI BROUGHT A PLEASED SMILE TO MY LIPS, AND I'D BE eternally grateful to him.

The following two days were uneventful and tedious, but it was tolerable thanks to Boone's delightful and loving company. Once I reached the thumb area in Michigan, I stopped at a small inn near the town where I'd soon be living, as it was late and I was exhausted.

The scenery before me was breathtaking. There were massive pine trees, stately oaks, and many blooming wildflowers. After inhaling deeply, I smelled the lake, pine, and the wonderfully clean and sweet air. Unfortunately, I couldn't see Lake Huron from here, but it was about a mile north of this motel.

The motel office door jingled as Boone and I entered, and I had to ring the small bell at the reception desk as no one appeared to be around. After waiting a minute or two, a fifteen-year-old girl trotted through the rear door. Her long red hair was in tight braids, and her hazel eyes smiled with friendliness. She wore a pink t-shirt that advertised one of the current grunge bands, and her shorts were wet and dirty. After wiping her hands on her stained clothes, she grabbed a clipboard and began writing. I leaned forward, rested my elbows on the counter, and gave her a kind smile.

Looking back up at me, she said, "Sorry 'bout that. I was cleaning some freshly caught trout and Chinook Salmon on the back porch. I'm hoping we can grill them for dinner tonight." At that moment, I caught the pungent smell of fish and wrinkled my nose.

She giggled at my expression and said, "Don't worry, you'll get used to the fishy smell—eventually." Her mischievous smile tickled my funny bone, and I grinned back.

"Not a problem. By the way, this is Boone. I hope you don't mind that I have a dog staying with me." Boone sat close beside me with his front paw resting on my toes.

"Nah. I love dogs. Our two are running around here somewhere...." She glanced out of the front window, obviously looking for her pets. "Hmm. They must be with Uncle Joe. He takes them with him when he has to run to town. But don't worry about 'em. They love people and other animals. You stayin' only one night?" I nodded in agreement. "If you'll just sign here." She popped her chewing gum and handed me the clipboard.

After I finished check-in, Boone and I drove to our rented unit. We settled in, and I decided on a hot shower to ease my achy muscles. Boone stayed on the bathroom rug while I bathed, and he immediately fell asleep. After carefully maneuvering around the dog as I stepped out of the shower,

I padded to the foggy mirror, wiped it with a towel, and gazed at my reflection.

I always wondered why people in my past called me beautiful. Wanting to see what others saw in my appearance, I tried to gauge my looks with an unbiased eye. My figure wasn't bad, although it was a little on the thin side —not surprising after what I had been through the past few months. I had a heart-shaped face, wide-set brown eyes, nicely shaped dark eyebrows, and thick lashes. My nose was small, and my mouth was slightly large. My skin always had a deeply tanned look, but that was because of my dad. He'd been African-American and a handsome one at that. My mom had been half Japanese-American, a quarter Indonesian, and the rest white. I was a culmination of all of them. My height was around five-foot-five, and I always wished I'd been taller. My dad had been well over six feet, but I stayed around my mom's height.

I pulled a brush through my hair, which came down below my shoulder blades and was heavily highlighted with blonde tints. The long dark brown hair that used to be down to my hips was now gone, and I was glad. It had been a lot of work, and it was what initially drew Trace to me—so he said. I guess my looks were okay, but I still had no clue what others saw in me. Since Trace started abusing me, I ceased wearing make-up or anything that could draw him to me, making me look younger than my twenty-six years.

Donning my usual nightshirt, I stirred Boone from his slumber, and we went to bed. It was only around seven, but I was exhausted and only wanted to sleep. Tomorrow was another day of possibilities, and I looked forward to seeing my new home.

THE NEXT DAY DAWNED BRIGHT AND CLEAR, AND EXCITEMENT FILLED ME AT seeing my new home at the cottage by the lake. Boone and I ate breakfast, then we headed out of the motel and into the car. My first stop was the lawyer. I finally saw beautiful Lake Huron as I drove toward his address. The water was deep blue, and the top of the waves glistened with the reflection of the bright morning sun. Boone thrust his head out the passenger window and sniffed the air with delight.

I entered the small town and stopped at a gas station for a fill-up.

Boone barked that he needed to relieve himself, so I let him trot over to the grassy area near the rear of the station. There was only one other vehicle at the establishment, and it was an old, heavy-duty red pickup that had many construction tools piled in the bed. I spied paint cans, ladders, and a plethora of things I had no clue as to their use. The driver was nowhere in sight, so I assumed he or she must be inside the store, and hoped Boone would remain the perfect gentleman he'd been the last several days.

Topping off the tank and finishing the sale, I heard a loud, angry male yell. Boone had disappeared. I heard his bark, and I hurried over, honing in on the location of the ruckus.

"Boone, where are you?" I hollered shakily.

As I turned the corner of the store, I spotted him. He stood before a tall man wearing a red baseball cap, and Boone had him backed up against the men's room door. My dog had him trapped, and Boone growled and danced around the man's feet, obviously not letting the poor guy move. Seeing the man's glowering expression, I knew I was in trouble.

"Boone! Bad dog! What's gotten into you, boy? Get over here!" I demanded in a no-nonsense tone. Boone glanced at me in guilt, then sidled over to the man, raised his leg, and peed on the poor guy's work pants. I heard the man swear in astonishment, but he was wise not to anger the dog further.

"Darn it, Boone! What's with you anyway?" He finally returned to my side, sat down, and smiled gleefully. "I'm so sorry. I've never seen him do that before—although I've only had him for over a week."

The man backed away from the door and shook the urine off his pant leg. Sweeping off his ball cap, he stuffed it into his pocket and ran a hand through his thick, dark hair. He carefully strode over to me and gave me a thunderous glare.

As I returned his stare, I inhaled a deep, shocked breath. *This male was gorgeous!* I couldn't say a word and stared at his magnificence. He was at least six-four, around thirty years old, broad-shouldered, and there wasn't an ounce of fat on his fantastic body. The paint-stained t-shirt hugged a muscled chest, and his well-developed biceps also drew my gaze. Then I glanced at the tattoo on the upper right arm. I assumed it was military, as it depicted a bald eagle atop an anchor and a sideways fork—a triton, I believe. His short, thick black hair framed a ruggedly handsome face. This was no pretty boy, but he oozed sex appeal. Those brown eyes appeared almost black, and his dark brows were lowered over an intense gaze as he stared at me in reprimand. His square jaw was chiseled yet clenched in restraint. I observed an elegant nose that had been broken at some point, a full sensual mouth, and a deep cleft in his strong chin. There was a five-o'clock shadow on his virile face, and he was deeply tanned from his extended time working outside in the summer sun.

"That dog is a menace, young lady. You'd better be careful because people around here don't take kindly to vicious dogs, and someone may shoot him if you're not more careful," he growled in a deep voice, and it rumbled through his chest. Even though I thought he was the cat's meow, I took great offense at the comment.

"How dare you!" I poked my finger into his chest with every word of my tirade. "He's just a pup, an abused one at that—and don't ever threaten this poor animal!" I moved to glare directly into the man's face. As I tried to stand taller, I stared unblinkingly into those dark, sensual eyes.

The man didn't back down from my onslaught, but he tilted his head as he peered into my eyes, clenched his jaw once more, then pulled me against his chest and kissed me. It was a brief kiss, but then again, a hot one. He set me away from him and stormed off toward the big red truck. He turned to pierce me with another steamy look, got in, and drove off, squealing his tires as he pulled back onto the road.

I stood there, breathing hard. After a moment, I glanced at Boone. He watched me while tilting his head back and forth.

"What!? Sure, you attack the man when he's leaving the john, then when he manhandles me, you do nothing but stare. What kind of a guard dog are you?"

"Arf!"

I raised my arms in exasperation, moved left, right, and left again. For some reason, I couldn't seem to think clearly.

"Men! They're useless and a total pain in the butt! Boone, get in the car!" I pointed my finger toward my vehicle. Somehow, this man ruined my good mood, and for some reason, my heart pounded loudly in my chest.

Slamming the driver's door after we got into the car, I sat there muttering in anger, frustration…and something else. Taking a soda out of the small cooler on the passenger side floor, I pressed the cold can against my cheek, then took a large swig and waited for my blood pressure to return to normal.

"That horrible, arrogant, insufferable son-of-a-gun! I hope he gets what's coming to him." I finally calmed down and put the car into gear. But for some reason, a grin spread across my face.

Chapter Five

As Boone and I continued driving through the small town, I scanned addresses for the attorney's office. I found it nestled between a laundromat and a title company. Leaving the windows partially down for Boone to stay cool, I entered the office. An older gentleman with a full head of graying hair and a ponytail greeted me.

"Hello. What can I do ya for?" he asked as he shook my hand firmly.

"I'm Hannah Renault. I believe you were expecting me this week?"

"Oh yes! So, you're Hannah! I'm Stanley Merrick. It's a pleasure to meet you, miss. After all our phone calls and texts, it's finally great to speak with you in person. By the way, how is Kogi? It was so good of him to initially handle your affairs for you."

"It was very nice of him, and he's doing great. Kogi sends his regards."

"He's such a kind man, and he admires you, my dear." I lowered my head and felt my face flush. Then, he asked, "I suppose you'd like to get down to business?"

"I would. I'm anxious to see Storm Harbor Cottage in person."

"You're going to love it. Especially since the renovation. Come, come, have a seat."

I took the cushy chair across from his desk and waited for him to continue.

"Hannah, I'll need to see a photo I.D.—I hope you understand."

"Of course." I dug out my new driver's license and handed it over. Biting my lip, I hoped he wouldn't question my identification or I'd be in big trouble.

He gazed at the photo and back at me. "That's you. Thanks! Now we can get down to the nitty-gritty." A thick file sat on his desk, and he pulled it open to shuffle through the contents. "I need your John Hancock on these final papers. Before you sign, let me call in my assistant so she can witness your signature." After calling her in, he made introductions, and we finished the legalities. "Everything else was already completed, so there isn't anything more I need from you.

"Regarding the cottage itself, all the upkeep, taxes, and insurance are covered under the estate provisions of the Will. Any updates or further renovations will be at your expense. As you know, the cottage rests on ten acres, and a substantial amount of lake frontage is included in that acreage."

"I understand. Stanley, can you tell me anything about the person who left me this cottage? I'm stumped as to why I was chosen as the inheritor."

"Hannah, under the conditions of the Will, I can't disclose their identity. All I know is that you are the one designated as the beneficiary, and I wasn't given the reason for this person's choice—nor is it any of my business."

I nodded my head after his comment and waited for him to continue. *But who could have left me such a valuable asset, and why?*

Stanley cleared his throat and continued, "On to another subject—my client left a substantial allowance for you to spend however you wish. Here's the first monthly check, and the payments can be directly deposited into any account you choose."

"What!?" I blurted a little too loudly when I saw the amount on the check. "There must be some mistake—I don't understand any of this."

"Hannah, there's no error—trust me. One thing I knew about your benefactor is there are no mistakes—they made sure of it, so there wouldn't be any hiccups when you received this inheritance. Once you settle in, there are a couple of banks down the street, or if you prefer, there are branches of larger bank chains in Port Austin." I nodded in shock, and he waited until I focused on his face again.

He handed me a large envelope and said, "I've provided everything you need to know about the cottage, the town, local businesses, etcetera. You're new to the area, and I know settling into an unfamiliar community can be difficult. But I want you to know the people of this town are good souls and will welcome you with open arms." He chuckled briefly, then continued, "Of course, there are always a few oddballs in every area—and we have ours. You'll meet our designated bad-attitude person soon enough, but he's harmless. Do you have any questions?"

"I think I met him this morning. He was rude and full of himself."

"Really? I'm sure Gus is out fishing all day," Stanley said with a look of confusion.

"Nope. My dog was a little aggressive with this man, and then he drove off in a huff in his big red truck."

Stanley chuckled, then replied, "That wasn't Gus, so you must be referring to Cade. He's the only one around here with a red truck. He does a lot of construction and is also a handyman. Cade's the one who did all the remodeling of Storm Harbor Cottage. Is this guy a very tall and handsome galoot with black hair and brown eyes?"

"Yep. That's him."

"I don't get it. He's a nice guy—quiet at times, maybe, but not mean, and I find that very strange."

"I guess I must have caught him on a bad day. Anyway, regarding any questions—I'll have to let you know, Stanley. It's a lot to take in at the moment."

We both stood and he shook my hand.

"You have my number, so don't hesitate to call if you think of anything."

I thanked him for his kindness and returned to my car. As I drove through the town, it had everything a person could possibly need. That was good to know since I hoped to stay close to home and keep my exposure to the locals at a minimum.

Following Stanley's directions, I drove down a long, paved road and found the turnoff. It was a dirt road but well-tended, and I kept traveling until I came to a long driveway with a sign that read, "Storm Harbor Lane." As I arrived at the cottage, the view was stunning. The house sat atop a small hill with an attached garage. I pulled up the driveway and stopped. Boone paced excitedly and turned in circles in the passenger seat.

"Okay, boy, just hold your horses."

I exited the car and opened his door. He bounded out and sniffed everything in sight. I laughed as he chased a chipmunk around a large oak tree. The chipmunk seemed to enjoy the game and kept circling the tree, causing Boone to become dizzy as he followed the animal in vain.

Leaving him to his antics, I strolled around the outside of the cottage. The size of my new home was much larger than I'd imagined. It was a three-story with what appeared to be a small attic space on the third floor. The outside of the place was sided in a pale blueish-gray color, with huge windows on the lower two levels that faced the lake. The spacious side yard was lovely. I was also surprised by the huge barn to the right of the cottage, and it matched the color of the home. It looked relatively new, and I decided to explore its interior later.

Returning to the cottage, I entered the front door. It opened into an impressive great room with high beamed ceilings. I could see through to the living area and the fantastic view of the back deck and the lake. Boone bounded in behind me and ran from room to room, obviously excited about his new home.

The place was painted in neutral colors, but the sofas, chairs, pillows, and decorations were in warm, cozy hues of burnt orange, gold, and turquoise. A large kitchen was straight ahead, and I had to check it out as well. The cabinets were white, while the flooring matched the living area's hardwood laminate. Granite countertops gleamed under the lights, and the center island was spacious and included a farmhouse sink and a dishwasher. The appliances were new and appeared to be expensive. *Wow!* Peeking inside, I saw the cabinets were fully stocked with everything I would need and plenty of staples to keep me supplied for a while.

Walking from room to room, I couldn't believe how beautiful everything was. I expected the cottage I inherited to be an old, rundown, roach-infested, dilapidated two-room shack. Instead, this magnificent home was beyond anything I could have imagined.

Moving on, I went up the stairs to the second floor to explore the primary bedroom, which took my breath away. It also had massive windows facing the lake, which included a set of French doors that led to a balcony. This spacious bedroom was thoughtfully decorated, and the ensuite had a soaker tub, double sinks, and a walk-in shower. Moving through another door beside the master, I found an office with a large desk, wooden file cabinets, and even a window nook where you could sit and read or simply enjoy the view.

Two more bedrooms were on the second floor, as well as a Jack and Jill bathroom. I spied the small stairwell, which led to the third story. Climbing to the top, I entered what I assumed was the attic through a heavy hatch door. It was small but interesting, and I didn't know what it could be used for. It wasn't large enough to hold much in the way of storage, and it was sparsely furnished. A bare table sat in the center of the room, and a few more folding tables were stacked along one wall. When I looked out each window, it surprised me how far I could view the property. The panes seemed somewhat different, but I wasn't sure why. I saw the words "Promadyne Security Products" etched in small print on the lower edge of the glass.

"That's odd. I swear these windows are made of bulletproof glass. But why? Hmm."

Returning to the first floor, I strolled to the rear left side of the cottage, where there was the laundry/mud room and also a half bath. I discovered another bedroom and a full bath to the right of the great room. I gloried in my new home and couldn't believe this place was mine. It was shocking that it was fully furnished and decorated with my simple taste in design.

Unable to sit down due to my excitement, I opened the French doors that led to the outdoor deck. It was immense and included a large grill, a fire pit, a massive seating area, and a huge outdoor umbrella table. As I moved to the right of the deck, a separate enclosed area contained an outdoor shower.

The view of the lake caught my breath. There were a few scattered trees along the sides of the deck, but the beach was clear and full of soft sand. Boone ran down the deck steps to the water and chased the waves as they bounded to the shore. The sun glistened off the water, and I took a moment to breathe in the scent of Lake Huron. As I inhaled, I caught the sweet smell of the roses that surrounded the sides of the deck and the bittersweet scent of the pine trees from the outer woods.

Boone's antics on the beach must have worn him out. He panted hard as he returned to my side, but a contented doggy smile peered at me. I patted his head, and he twisted his body in a circle in a loving response.

"Come on, boy. Let's get a bite to eat. What do you say?" He barked happily, and we returned inside the cottage.

For the remainder of the day, I unpacked my few belongings and made a list of things I'd need from town. That evening, we watched the big screen television and caught up on the news, then watched some old sitcoms. All too soon, my eyes grew heavy, and we went upstairs and turned in for the night. Opening the large doors, I closed the screen, and the warm, lake-scented breeze wafted in. I could hear the gentle *whap, whap* of the waves teasing the sandy shore. A bright moon beamed over the vast water of the lake. Boone slept in his usual position, snuggled next to me.

As I waited for sleep, I couldn't help thinking how blessed I was to receive this fantastic new home. But on the other hand, I knew my good fortune wouldn't last. It was only a matter of time before the danger I'd been running from would soon catch up with me. It always did.

Chapter Six

The next morning, I woke to something wet licking my face.

"Ewe, Boone, that is quite a rude awakening, bub." He stared intently into my eyes, and it was apparent he'd been waiting impatiently for me to give him breakfast. I pulled Boone close and kissed the top of his head.

He ran ahead of me down the stairs, and I let him out the side door of the mud room where he could relieve himself in the grassy side yard. He didn't take long and quickly returned and trotted up the steps and back into the laundry room. It made me wonder if I should have an area fenced on this side of the cottage, so I wouldn't have to worry about Boone running off. I'd ask Stanley about it, as well as a recommendation for a veterinarian.

Padding around in the kitchen barefoot, I prepared Boone's breakfast. He gratefully accepted his bowl of food, and as I watched him eat, I realized his once undernourished body was beginning to fill out, and his coat had a glossy sheen. The few bald patches were already covered with new soft fur.

Boone finished his food and took a long drink from the water dish. He ran to the great room, where I had piled several of his toys in one corner, and grabbed his favorite purple pot-bellied pig. Jumping onto the sofa, he gnawed on the legs.

"I'm going to take a long shower and get ready for the day, baby. Enjoy your piggy." At my comment, he bit down hard on the toy's body, and it let out a loud and nauseating squeal. He thought it was hilarious and kept making it squeak. I ran upstairs to escape the assault on my ears.

That afternoon, I left Boone safely home and drove back to town. I'd need a few more groceries, dog food, and some personal items, plus I hoped to stop in to see Stanley. It didn't take long to pick up my supplies, and when I pulled up to the lawyer's office, I spotted the big red truck parked in the same lot. I hoped that awful man wasn't with Stanley because I didn't feel like dealing with him today. But for some reason, I continued looking around for him as I walked to the office door.

Stanley was at his desk, and luckily he was alone in his office. He greeted me with surprise and asked me to sit.

"How's it going, Hannah? Is everything to your satisfaction?"

"And then some! I had no idea the place would be so amazing, Stanley. It's spectacular! I still don't understand it all, but I'll enjoy it while the getting's good." I giggled, and the sound coming from my mouth surprised me. I'm not generally a "giggly" female.

"Trust me, kiddo. It's all yours—free and clear."

"I'm still pinching myself. Stanley, I'd like to install a small fenced-in area for my dog, Boone. Can you recommend someone who could do the work? I also need a vet for him as well."

"For the fence, Cade is my vote as he does most of the building, remodeling, and whatnot around here. He's reliable, knowledgeable, and reasonable. As for the vet, we only have one, but she's well-liked by both humans and beasts. Her name is Kelly Neumann. Let me get you their info."

As he rifled through his phone and wrote down their names and numbers, I cringed at the thought of dealing with this Cade fellow. I had the feeling we'd be like oil and water. Not good.

"Thanks, Stanley. I appreciate the help."

"Anytime, Hannah, and if there's anything else I can do ya for, just let me know."

With a wave, I departed Stanley's office and wondered if I would catch a glimpse of Cade in town. *What?* I couldn't believe I was looking for him. *What's wrong with me?* I hate men as a rule—especially young, attractive ones. You've never been relationship material, either. *Get a grip, girl!*

Using Stanley's directions, I strolled down to the vet's office and spoke with the receptionist. I told her about Boone and his situation, and she made an appointment for us for the following week.

The man called Cade was across the street speaking with an old man who sat on a bench outside the barbershop. I heard their laughter and decided to approach and ask Cade about his services. Taking a deep breath, I carefully crossed the street and walked up to them.

As I neared the two men, they scowled, and I almost backed away in fear. Even though I briefly faltered in my step, I thought about Kogi and continued on in determination.

"No dog today?" Cade asked in a wry tone.

"Nope. He's home and hopefully staying out of trouble." I decided to take the innocent tact and not give him an opening to insult Boone.

"That's good. Can I help you?"

The man was even better looking today if that was possible. He wore a clean short-sleeved gray sports shirt and tight black jeans. My knees felt weak, and I licked my lips in nervousness. I stared back for a moment, not saying a word.

"Well, speak up, woman! We don't have all day!" This exceedingly rude remark came from the old, ornery man on the bench.

"It's okay, Gus. I've got this," Cade replied, staring intently at me with one dark brow arched in question.

"I know we got off on the wrong foot yesterday, and for that, I'm sorry. I also apologize for Boone's behavior. It was very out of character and I don't know why he reacted that way."

He only said, "Apology accepted."

I tried my best not to grimace at his curt response and continued, "The reason I'm here is that Stanley gave me your name and said you're the one to speak with regarding construction. I'm hoping you could give me an estimate for installing a new fence around a small area of my newly acquired property."

He looked confused and asked, "I'm sorry, but I don't know who you are. What's your name and where's your property?"

"Oh my gosh, I'm sorry again. My name is Hannah Renault, and I'm the new owner of Storm Harbor Cottage."

The old man swore loudly, stood up stiffly, spat on the ground, and stalked off.

Cade quickly spoke up regarding the old man's rude behavior. "Don't worry about him. He isn't happy about the cottage going to a stranger. And he's always cranky. You'll get used to him. I'm Cade Copano, and welcome to our humble little town."

It surprised me when his face lit up with a bright smile, and he stood up and offered me his hand. His stunning grin caused a dimple to appear on the side of his mouth, and it made my heart beat faster with awareness. He shook my hand firmly and a *zing* went down to my toes. I had never experienced such an attraction and had no clue how to handle it.

"Thank...you...." I stammered. My palms began to sweat, and I felt like a stupid, innocent schoolgirl. I didn't like it one bit.

"I did most of the remodeling of the cottage. Which area are you looking to have fenced?" He motioned for me to sit, and I joined him on the bench.

"Uh...a space off the laundry room—it's for Boone...the dog?" I couldn't stop stammering.

"I see. That would be an excellent area for a dog fence. How about I stop over tomorrow morning, say around ten? I'll bring photos of different fencing styles that may work, and you can show me how big of an area you'd like enclosed. Will that work?" He smiled again, and at that moment, I wondered if he was being deliberately charming to throw me off my game. Trace used that maneuver to get what he wanted. I instantly stiffened but smiled back and decided to follow his lead.

"That would be great. I'll see you then." I stood and he politely joined me. Then, smiling flirtatiously, I turned around and walked away with a bit of a butt-wiggle. After climbing into my car, I glanced back at him and he stared in my direction. Luckily, I knew he couldn't see me through the darkened windows, so I could view him without him knowing. But the son-of-a-gun *did* know. He smiled that devil-may-care grin and waved in my direction. And stupid me, I waved back!

THE FOLLOWING DAY, I TOOK EXTRA CARE GETTING DRESSED AND EVEN applied makeup. I cursed at myself for caring, but it didn't stop me from trying to appear more attractive. Taking one last glance in the mirror, my behind looked tight and round in the snug blue jeans, and the purple tank top hugged my breasts. After throwing on some sneakers, a loud rumble of a vehicle echoed through the open windows. Running down the stairs, I heard a knock on the front door.

Boone barked, but I shushed him and told him to behave. I cautiously opened the door and Cade glanced around my feet. Boone sat silently beside me and wagged his tail excitedly at my guest.

"He likes me now?" Cade asked skeptically.

"I guess so. As I said before, he's generally very social. I've no clue why he behaved the way he did."

"Hmm."

I let him in, and Boone jumped up to greet our guest. Cade crouched down and smiled widely at him. After being petted, Boone ran across the room, picked up his purple pig, and brought it over to Cade.

"I guess you're now his best friend," I replied in confusion.

"I'm glad. He's a nice dog, although he seems a bit thin."

I explained how I came to be Boone's new, proud owner.

Cade smiled sincerely and said, "You did a very noble thing. Most people wouldn't care about a stray dog, much less chase him around for an hour and then take him to the vet."

My face flushed with embarrassment and I didn't know what to say. Cade noticed my discomfort and asked, "How about you show me where you'd like the fencing?"

"Yeah, sure." I led the way, Boone followed closely while carrying his pig, and he kept bumping the squeaky toy against the back of Cade's legs. When Cade stopped beside me in the side yard, I inhaled his intoxicating scent—a light, spicy aftershave and peppermint. It made my knees weak again. *Stop it! He's simply another man who'll hurt and destroy you!* My mind kept saying one thing, but my body was telling me something else.

I watched him as he walked around the area, took several measurements, and came to stand beside me—way too close. I loved it and hated it. Fear won over and I took one step away. He noticed but was polite not to comment. We returned inside the cottage and sat on the stools at the kitchen island.

"I have several photos of fencing I think would be excellent for a dog, yet wouldn't detract from the homey ambiance of the cottage's architecture and surrounding landscape." He pulled his stool closer to me and I felt the heat from his exquisite body. I went through the photos and tried to ignore my physical reaction to his presence, good and bad. This man certainly knew his job. Any of the fences would work and still add charm to the place and not look like an eyesore.

After selecting one, he complimented me on my choice. "That's what I would've chosen. By the way, what do you think of the place? I had to do a complete gut and remodel, but I thought it turned out well. It was difficult to gauge what the next owner would like without ever meeting them." His question wasn't asked in an arrogant tone, and I answered honestly.

"I love it and think everything is perfect. The design, colors, furnishing, plants, flowers—everything is exactly what I would've wanted. You have excellent taste, Cade. Thank you, and I mean that sincerely." I offered my hand again and he took it warmly. The undeniable attraction to him reared its ugly head.

"You're very welcome. Just let me know if you'd like anything changed." The phone on his hip vibrated; he glanced at it, then turned his attention back to me. "I'll order the fencing and I should be able to get started next week. Is that okay?"

"Sure. That would be great, thanks. By the way, do you know if there's Internet set up here?"

"Yes. It's bundled with the cable T.V. If you need a computer, there's a great shop in town. Just ask for Huey and tell him I sent you—he'll take good care of you." We stood up and went to the door. Boone was still close to Cade's heels and continued pushing the pig against the back of Cade's knees. He laughed and scratched Boone's ears, which made the dog smile with happiness.

Cade bent down and said, "I'm glad we're now friends, Boone. And I'm also happy your mom and I are too." Cade looked up at me and gave me another friendly smile. I felt that pull again and I didn't like it, but I still returned a shy smile. It was impossible not to stare at him as he walked away. His muscles flexed as he climbed into his truck and waved as he departed.

Craning my neck, I stared at his vehicle until it disappeared from view. I didn't know I'd been gawking until I heard my involuntary sigh.

"Honestly, Boone, you'd think I'd never seen a good-looking man before. Sheesh!" Boone tilted his head at me, and I continued, "I can tell you right now, bub, he's not on the menu for this young woman. No, siree!" Boone looked at me with an expression of disbelief, and he even had the gall to shake his head in response.

"Aww, what do you know anyway, you silly mutt?" I asked as I patted his head. But in my mind, all I heard was, *I wonder if Cade likes me.*

Chapter Seven

The next day, Boone and I went back into town. I needed to set up a bank account, deposit the inheritance check, and then stop at the computer store. After finding a nice shaded parking spot, I lowered the windows and told Boone to stay. I selected a bank and set up all of my banking needs.

As I strolled to the computer store, I was unlucky enough to pass by Gus on the sidewalk. He deliberately blocked my way with his scrawny old body, hoping to intimidate me. I went to sidestep him, but he was spry for an old man and stood before me again.

I stopped, crossed my arms, and glared at the offending octogenarian. "Do you think you scare me, old man? It'll take more than the likes of you to intimidate me. Now, move out of my way, you old buzzard!" My words startled him, and he hurriedly stepped aside while staring at me with surprise.

But as I moved away, I heard him grumble, "Thief!"

I rolled my eyes and entered the store. After asking for Huey, a kind, shy young man of about nineteen with red hair, freckles, and acne stood before me. We shook hands and I told him Cade recommended him. He beamed with pride that Cade thought so highly of him, and he gushed with excitement. I found Huey to be sweet and exceptionally knowledgeable about computers. Even though I knew exactly what I wanted and needed, I listened intently to his advice and pondered his suggestions. He also helped me select a new cell phone and set it up for me. His confidence boomed when I thanked him for his assistance and purchased everything I needed for my home office. The young man even asked if I required help setting things up at the cottage.

"Thanks, Huey, but I think I'll be fine. However, I know who to call if I get into trouble. You're the man, my friend." I gave him a fist bump and he glowed with pride and happiness. He helped me stow my purchases in the trunk, and Boone admired Huey as well. Boone gave him a lick on the cheek and a paw on Huey's arm. I thanked the boy again and drove toward the cottage.

As I neared my property, I saw someone walking along the side of the road. As I neared the person, I discovered it was an older woman around sixty years old. I pulled alongside her and asked if she'd like a ride. The lady bent over to gaze at me and gave me a charming smile.

"Well, actually, dear, I'd love one. I normally like to take long walks, but my arthritis has decided to flare up." I pulled over to the side of the road and she climbed in beside me. Boone, who'd been in the back seat, placed his paws on the top of the front seat and smiled at the older woman.

She jumped slightly and said, "Oh my, I didn't expect you, handsome."

"I'm sorry. I should've mentioned Boone. Is he a problem?"

"Not at all. He just surprised me, that's all. I love animals." She stroked Boone's head and crooned gently to him. He loved her.

For being in her sixties, this woman was stunning. She was tall with a slim figure, her face had a regal elegance, and her eyes were large, dark brown, and expressive. I had the impression she was of Native American heritage because of her strong, dignified facial structure—prominent high cheekbones, well-shaped jaw, and a radiant, warm skin tone. Her chin-length, straight black hair was weaved with silver strands that appeared elegantly placed by Mother Nature.

"I'm Hannah Renault." I offered her my hand and she shook it with a firm, yet gentle grip.

"Nice to meet you, dear. You can call me Lois. You're new around here, aren't you?"

"Yes. I've only been here a couple of days. I now live at Storm Harbor Cottage."

"Really? I heard a lot of renovation was done to that place."

"I guess so. It's absolutely beautiful, though I never saw it before it was redone."

"Hmm," was all she said.

"Where can I drop you, Lois?"

"Just let me out at the crossroad ahead, Hannah. I'm feeling better, and the doctor said I have to exercise every day or my joints lock up."

"Are you sure? Do you have to walk far to return home?" I pulled over and stopped the car.

"Nope. I'll be fine, dear." She squeezed my arm in thanks and patted Boone on the head. "Thanks for the ride. You've been very kind."

"Any time, Lois. Will I see you again?"

"Definitely. Now that I've met you, try and keep me away—if you don't mind being friends with an old woman."

"You're not old...I mean, you're older than me, but not old...I guess...." I seemed to have developed the habit of rambling and making a fool of myself. Looking away, I attempted to hide my blushing face.

I heard boisterous laughter beside me, and when I peered at her, she snickered even more. When I saw the comical look on her face, I couldn't help myself and went into gales of giggles. I didn't know why I found the situation so funny, but it felt freeing to laugh again.

"Thanks, Lois. I haven't laughed like that since...actually, I can't remember when I ever laughed like that." For some reason, I already loved this woman and felt like we were instant friends.

"Me either, Hannah. You're a gem and I'm so happy to have met you." She exited the car and shut the door. She glanced through the open window again and said, "I'll see the two of you very soon."

"I hope so, Lois. Later!" I pulled away and Boone even barked goodbye to her.

AFTER RETURNING HOME, SETTING UP THE COMPUTER AND PRINTER DIDN'T take long. I was well on my way to starting my new career. The VPN was also in place, so I hoped it was enough protection to save me from prying eyes.

As a child and a budding teenager, I loved writing stories. I wanted to start writing again, and fiction was my favorite. Several ideas were roaming through my mind, and I hoped I could bring them to fruition.

My husband had seen some of my manuscripts but told me they were stupid and I was a lousy writer. Unbeknownst to him, I'd already sent them to an agent, and she wanted to represent me. I'd also saved my two completed novels on the Cloud where he couldn't find them. But once Trace took away any access to a computer, my dream of being published dissolved. After I contacted the agent and told her I couldn't pursue writing at the moment, she told me to contact her if I ever changed my mind. Needless to say, I ceased the one joy that had allowed me to escape his reign of terror over me, but I still kept the agent's business card.

But now, things were different. Becoming a successful writer was back in my future. So I downloaded my two novels from the Cloud to my laptop and started reviewing them joyfully.

"Screw you, Trace!" I said with finality.

THAT AFTERNOON, BOONE AND I WENT FOR A WALK. I WANTED TO EXPLORE the barn and the ten acres surrounding the property. As I approached the outbuilding, I spotted a small structure a short distance away. It had a large smoke stack through the roof. Cords of wood were stored a few feet away from this strange building.

"I wonder what this is for, my boy. Any ideas?" Boone tilted his head at my question but turned around and walked up to the gigantic barn as if he knew where I wanted to go.

I had no idea why someone would want a building this large on lake property, but I figured they must have had a reason. As I walked around the outside, it appeared enormous—and it even had two stories. Several windows surrounded each level, allowing plenty of light to enter the barn. I spotted one regular pedestrian door at one end, and on each side of the more expansive outer walls were two huge sliding doors. A double garage door and a cement pad had been installed at the other end of the barn. *Was this barn designed for machinery of some kind?*

"Come on, Boone, let's check it out." I couldn't wait to see what was inside. Once I opened the service door, Boone took off at a full run to explore the building's contents. Searching for a light switch, I found several along the right side of the entrance. Flipping them on, the barn lit up like a Christmas Tree.

"Goodness gracious—it's enormous!" The center floor of the barn contained dirt, but there were cement walkways along the rooms against the outer walls that looked like large stalls. I entered the first two, and they appeared to be large animal enclosures with built-in feeding stations in one corner—horse stalls, maybe? Each stall had an outer door. I opened one and saw a large, fenced-in pasture. Closing the door again, I went to the next room. This area had several shelves on each wall, which contained animal cages of every shape and size. The next one also had spots for storage, and there were a few bags of pine shavings, a couple bales of green hay, and a bag of wildfowl feed. Another shelf had canned kitten and adult cat food, a bag of cat kibble, kitty litter, and a pan. *How strange.*

A large area had been walled off from the rest of the building at the other end of this massive barn. After entering through the door, I realized this was where the garage door had been located; it looked as if it was set up for an auto mechanic. There weren't any tools yet, but there were several storage areas and even a hoist. I left and returned to the center of the building. The remainder of the barn was open, and I assumed it could be turned into whatever the new owner desired. *But why all the animal enclosures and stalls? Hmm.*

As I had assumed earlier, this barn and all the equipment were brand, spanking new. I looked above my head and had to investigate what was on the second story. There were two sets of stairs—one on each side of the barn. Boone followed me up, and there were wood floors and tall, sturdy railings along each side of the upper story. One large area was built over the two horse stalls I assumed was for hay storage. A small hatch was on the outer wall of this area for a hay elevator. The remainder of the upper floor was left open. The barn was insulated, and vents were spaced along the upper and lower floors. *Is this fantastic barn heated? Is that what the separate small building was for—to burn wood for heat? I'll have to ask Cade.*

"Boone, what do you think, boy?" He barked with excitement and we returned to the first floor. He ran around and around and was having a ball. After several minutes, my pup finally stopped and flopped down on the floor in a spread-eagled sploot.

"Are you done with your zoomies, Boone?"

He smiled with happiness and replied, "Arf, arf!"

"I guess so. We'll wait a few minutes and then walk around the property." I sat beside him on the cement and waited until he rested.

We walked out of the barn and started our tour of the property. There appeared to be well-defined trails and the woods were relatively clean. It was a gorgeous stroll among the pines, oaks, and poplars. We encountered all kinds of wildlife, which thrilled Boone. I was surprised he didn't chase any of them, but only watched them with fascination.

Finally, we turned toward the house but altered our course and meandered to the beach. I sat near the shore, kicked off my shoes and socks, and buried my toes in the warm sand. Boone trotted to the lake, jumped a few times when the waves touched his toes, then bravely and cautiously entered the water for a long drink. When he had his fill, he returned to lie down beside me. I followed his lead and laid back against the soft ground.

The sun warmed my body and the cool breeze of the lake caressed my skin. Before I knew it, I bolted awake and sat up. Glancing at my watch, I discovered Boone and I had been asleep for over an hour. But I'd never felt so rested and at peace. Boone nuzzled my arm and looked at me questioningly.

"Yes, it's your dinnertime. Let's go."

After I fed Boone, I received a call from Cade. "Hello, Cade. What can I do for you?"

"Hi, Hannah. I hope you're doing well."

"I am, thanks."

"I wanted to give you the total cost for the fencing job. I usually require a deposit. Will that work for you?"

"That'll be fine. What's the damage?" I laughed, and he chuckled on the other end. He told me the total price and what he required for the down payment.

After agreeing to the amount, I asked, "Can I write you a check?"

"That'll work, but I thought we could kill two birds with one stone, so to speak. Would you like to join me for dinner tonight? I wanted to give you the low-down on the town and everyone in it, good and bad. What do you say?"

I didn't answer immediately because he surprised me with the invitation.

"Hannah?"

"Uh, sorry. You took me by surprise. Y—es. Where and at what time?"

"There's an excellent Italian restaurant called Santino's I thought you might like. It's downtown, just off Main Street on Hollis Avenue. Just turn right where Martin's Coins is located. You can't miss it. How does six-thirty sound?"

"That'll work. Don't worry; I'll leave Boone at home." I accidentally snorted, and my face flushed with embarrassment.

"Hannah! You're a snorter! I love it!" He chuckled loudly, and I couldn't help myself and laughed along with him.

"Sorry about that," I apologized, still giggling. "I've never done that before and have no clue why I did."

"I think it's charming. There's another call coming in and I have to answer it. I'll see you tonight. Goodbye, Hannah."

"Bye, Cade."

I hung up the phone and my hands were cold and clammy as I thought about meeting him. "Come on, Hannah, don't be ridiculous. He's a man, and remember, you don't like any of them," I mumbled.

Boone barked, telling me he had to go out to take care of business. He took off like a shot out of the mud room, and he spent so much time trying to find the right place to poop I finally said, "Don't run off, Boone. I need to get the casserole out of the oven." I'd already prepared a meal for myself, but I didn't want to tell Cade. For some reason, I wanted to meet him for a nice dinner. Pulling the meal from the oven, I let it cool on the counter.

I rushed back to the door, figuring Boone would be waiting to come in.

However, he wasn't there. Scanning the yard, I tried to find him, but he was nowhere in sight.

"Boone! Come!" I waited for several minutes, but he didn't return. Walking outside, I scurried around the entire side yard and repeatedly called him, but he still didn't appear. "Dang it, Boone!"

At least he had on his bright red collar, so hopefully, if someone found him, they'd know he had an owner. Biting my lip, tears pooled in my eyes.

I called him repeatedly, frantically running around the woods, but he never returned. With my head hung low and shoulders drooping, I eventually returned to the cottage. I repeatedly searched for him several times throughout the rest of the afternoon, screaming his name around the outside of the cottage.

It was time for me to get ready for my date with Cade. I could only think about Boone, but I braided my hair, carefully applied makeup, and selected a print sundress and delicate heels. After inserting small silver hoop earrings in my ears and a delicate matching chain around my neck, I rushed downstairs to try again to find Boone. Opening the side door, I spotted him coming toward me. He looked tired and not in the least bit apologetic.

"Boone! I'm so relieved you're home, but where the heck have you been? You scared me to death!"

He stopped several feet away, then glanced behind him.

"Come on, boy. I need you to come in."

Refusing to move, he looked back toward the woods again. I waited, wondering what he was doing. After several minutes, there was movement in the ferns, and a cat strolled out and moved to sit beside Boone.

"What the...." Boone barked once, and then the cat let out a pitiful meow—it was more of a squeak.

Boone moved toward me and so did the cat. Apparently, Boone had a new friend—and an unseemly one. The poor thing was underweight, had missing patches of hair, and the remaining fur was matted with burrs. I supposed it could be considered pretty if it hadn't been in such a mess, plus half of one ear was missing. It had long since healed, so apparently, this kitty had been in the wild for some time. Boone and the feline strolled around me and entered the house.

"Crap!" I quickly closed the door and trotted after the duo. I found them in the kitchen, and the cat was drinking from Boone's water bowl. He sat to the side, waiting for the kitty to quench its thirst.

When the mangy thing finished, it strolled over to me and rubbed against my leg. I could hear its loud purr, and I crouched down to get a better look at the stray. Petting it lightly, I could feel its ribs. The feline moved back and forth, and I looked at his butt. It was a male, though I had no clue whether he'd been neutered—I had no experience with cats. He rolled over, showing me his belly. His fur was primarily black, but he had a white mustache, a white chest, and matching white socks. Even with his bald patches, he had a full mane, and his tail looked as if it had long hair. When I stared at his feet, he appeared to have extra toes.

"What am I going to do with you, kitty?" He responded with a husky chirp. The poor thing needed some food. "Give me a few minutes, fella." I just remembered there was cat food in the barn.

I found the kibble on the shelf and checked the expiration date.

"Eureka!"

Bringing in a few cans of wet food and the bag of kibble, I opened one of the tins and spooned a small amount into a bowl. The cat devoured it and wanted more.

"Hold on, baby. Let that settle first."

I checked my watch and I still had a half hour before I needed to leave. After waiting fifteen minutes, I gave the kitty another helping, then put the cooled casserole into the fridge.

"What am I going to do with you while I'm gone, cat?" I thought for several minutes, then decided to lock Boone and the cat in the laundry room. I piled some towels on the floor and remembered there was litter and a pan in the barn. After retrieving them, I settled the two animals in the room. Boone laid down next to the kitty while the mangy newcomer bathed. They both seemed content, and it was time for me to leave for my date.

"I'm trusting the two of you to behave yourselves. I should be back in a couple of hours." After I kissed Boone, I patted the top of the cat's head. There was an "arf" and a "meow" as I left the cottage and climbed into the car.

Chapter Eight

I arrived five minutes late, but figured after all I had to do before leaving the cottage, I made excellent time. After entering the restaurant, I scanned the tables for Cade. We spotted each other simultaneously, and he waved in my direction.

When I reached the table, he stood and held my chair. I thanked him and sat down.

"Hannah, you look beautiful."

"Thank you. You look spiffy too." I blushed with embarrassment at his compliment and felt awkward and unsure.

"Spiffy, huh? Thanks." I knew he was teasing me, but I appreciated it.

He did look amazing—he always did. His undeniable rugged good looks and masculinity drew every woman's eye in the restaurant. He wore a pearl gray, silky button-down shirt and black trousers, which accentuated his dark, startling good looks. I detected his spicy, clean aftershave, and he had shaved for our date. His usual five o'clock shadow was gone. *I liked it.*

We were given a menu and ordered wine. Cade was attentive, kind, and thoughtful during dinner. The meal was delicious, and the wine was excellent. We kept the conversation light and noncommittal. I told him about Boone's new best friend, which was why I'd been late tonight. He chuckled at my caricature description of the cat, making me glad he found it amusing.

"Hannah, tell me about yourself."

My smile halted, and I lowered my eyes in frustration. After a couple of moments, which seemed like forever, I said, "Cade, I don't like talking about myself—especially my past. I hope you don't mind."

"You don't have to tell me. I don't talk about my military service either —it's not something I like to remember. But other than that, I'm an open book."

He scanned my face, then said, "I'll start. Thirty-one years ago, I was born in Bad Axe, Michigan, into a wonderful family. I'm close to my parents, sister, Delta, and brother, Phoenix. Phoenix is the oldest, and I'm the middle child. Delta's married with three adorable kids, and Phoenix is engaged to be married next June. I've never gotten hitched, nor am I currently dating anyone. My dad owns his own construction company, and that's how I learned everything about the trade. My mom's a successful veterinarian and is also a fantastic artist.

"I was raised Catholic, although I lapsed for a time while I was in the military. But since then, I've atoned and returned to the faith. I love working on and rebuilding old cars, but I haven't had time to pursue this passion. Don't worry. I also love animals and had many of them growing up. Did I leave anything out?"

"I wouldn't know...." I smiled impishly, then said, "What I can talk about is I love writing novels. I hope to earn a living from this venture, but it's early yet, and time will tell. I've already set up an office and a computer, and if it's in the cards, I can earn a decent living doing just that. We'll see. I also love animals but never had any growing up. As to family, I have none and am unattached." Although I knew this last statement was a bit of a lie, I kept trying to convince myself that it was so. "I'm not religious and don't believe in God." I watched his face when I said this, but there was no apparent reaction. With a relieved sigh, I continued, "Inheriting the cottage was a great surprise but a dream come true, although I've no clue who left it to me. Do you know?"

He looked at me strangely, then said, "You really have no idea?" I shook my head in denial. "I'm sorry to say, me neither. Stanley hired me to

64

do all the work on the cottage two years ago. There was a specific list of instructions from whoever left you the place, and I had to follow them to a tee. Right down to the type of cat food in the barn. I thought it was odd, but the pay was good and I thoroughly enjoyed the job."

"Really? You were told to put certain things in the barn?" I gave him a puzzled stare and thought about what he'd said. "Regarding the barn, were you also told to build a working garage too?"

"Yep."

"You don't say? That's so weird."

Cade nodded in agreement, and when the server appeared, we ordered dessert. He wanted Italian rum cake and I opted for classic tiramisu.

"Cade, what's that weird building behind the barn, and what's all the wood for?"

"That's an outdoor wood-burning hydronic furnace that uses wood to heat the barn. It gets freezing here in the winter, so whoever left you the property wanted you to be able to utilize the barn during the cold winter months."

"Wow, really? I wondered what those vents were for in the barn, and I hope you'll show me how to use the furnace before winter hits."

"You got it."

"Is the barn also set up for a couple of horses? I noticed the stalls and the outer doors that lead to a pasture. I'm very green regarding horses, so I wasn't sure."

"Yes. My instructions were to also provide a place for two horses and whatever else it may require. Luckily, I grew up with equines, so I knew what was needed."

"Cade, what do you like to do in your spare time?"

"Hmm. I'd say watching those famous old westerns. My grandfather loved black-and-white movies. So I grew up admiring the old-time actors —John Wayne, Jimmy Stewart, Henry Fonda, and the like. I still watch them."

"I like westerns too, but I've never seen those old ones. I'll have to check them out," I replied.

"Let me know—I'd love to watch them with you."

I smiled widely, happy to know he'd like to see me again. We sat in comfortable silence for a few moments, but I finally had to ask about the ornery geezer in town.

"Cade, what's up with Gus? Is he mean to everyone, or is it just me?"

"I can't say he likes anyone, at least, not as far as I know. Even though I've asked around about him, people don't say much about his attitude or life. The rumor is he wasn't always a cantankerous old man, and apparently, something tragic happened in his past, and afterward, he became impossible."

"But I saw the two of you talking and laughing. He must like you, Cade."

"He tolerates me and likes it when I tell him a funny joke—especially if it's slightly off-color. That's what you witnessed. Don't take it personally regarding his attitude toward you. He detests newcomers. I received the same treatment when I moved here, and it took months for him to stop the swearing and spitting when we encountered each other in town."

Dessert arrived and I savored the delicious confection. Halfway through devouring its sweetness, my fork stopped mid-air when I spotted Cade staring at my mouth. I gazed into his eyes and it was a mistake. There was a smoldering passion reflected in their depths, and I felt myself drowning in those dark brown pools. It made me squirm in my chair and I felt the heat pouring through my body. My breathing shallowed and I had no clue how to stop my reaction to this obvious attraction to one another. Laying down the fork, I took an unladylike gulp from my wine glass.

Cade had also stopped eating but stared at my face, then lower. With his simple look, my body reacted even stronger than before. *I have to stop this!*

"Cade, don't," I whispered urgently.

He sat back in his chair, looked away, and wiped his mouth with the cloth napkin. He said, "I'm sorry. However, I can't deny my attraction to you, Hannah. You're a stunning, beautiful, intelligent woman, and it's been a long time since I felt this way—if ever. I also can't shake the feeling that I have to get to know you better. Trust me, I don't understand it, but there it is."

"Cade..." I didn't know how to address my feelings or tell him I wasn't relationship material. But I had to say something. "I'm not what you're looking for. No matter how attracted we are to one another, it can't happen. My past is a mess and so am I. I'm damaged goods." After lowering my head, I took another sip of wine because I feared his response.

I heard nothing for a few minutes, but then a deep chuckle escaped Cade's lips. My resentful gaze met his and his laughter died quickly. He acknowledged my glare and apologized.

"Hannah, I'm not laughing at you, I'm laughing at our situation. Do you have any idea that I feel the same way about myself? I'm also damaged goods and was mean to you initially because I wanted to be near you as soon as we met. I was angry about how I felt and was in denial about my feelings for you. It made me crazy!"

I stared at him in shock and was mystified about why he felt that way about me.

"Hannah, the things I saw and had to do in the war screwed with my head. After serving in the military, I've been struggling with PTSD, nightmares, anxiety, confinement issues, and so on. But with a lot of help, I'm learning to deal with it. Now, do you understand?"

"I do. I'm so sorry, Cade." I giggled at the situation and how much we had in common. He began laughing with me, and I chuckled so hard I snorted again. That sent Cade into a fierce attack of guffaws, and I joined in. The other diners stared and it made us hoot even louder. By the time we calmed down, we had tears running down our cheeks.

"I guess we'd better leave before they kick us out," Cade said with a wink and asked the server for the check.

After paying for the meal and leaving a generous tip, he walked me to my car. He opened the door and guided me into the seat.

"I've never told you, but this is some rad car. Is it a 1970?"

"Uh-huh."

"Start it up, Hannah. I want to hear it running, please."

I turned the key in the ignition and let it roar, and then it idled down into its usual purr.

Cade's eyes were closed as he listened to the humming engine. He had a pleased expression, opened his eyes, and looked at me. "Got to love that 442."

"You definitely know cars." I smiled back at him in pride. "I'd better go. Who knows what those two animals have been up to in my laundry room."

He smiled and said, "They should be fine as long as they know to separate the whites from the darks."

I giggled at his comment, but the mood turned heavy and I stared hungrily at his mouth.

Cade leaned in and I held my breath. At that moment, I wanted nothing more than for him to kiss me. I closed my eyes and felt his lips touch mine, then the kiss deepened. Cade kept it gentle and sweet. But I couldn't contain myself, so I grabbed his shirt and pulled him closer, wanting to prolong the intimate contact. Cade's lips changed from gentleness to passion, and I followed him into the abyss of pleasure. I didn't want him to stop—ever. But he did. When I opened my eyes, he closed the car door and backed away. After rolling down the window, we looked at each other, our eyes locked in awareness. He smiled with a flirty, knowing grin, then walked away.

"Crap!" I muttered in frustration as I drove back to the cottage. This relationship can't happen, and I'm being delusional to even consider it a possibility. My growing feelings for Cade must be nipped in the bud starting now. Even with repeating my denials and negativity about Cade, I grinned the entire ride home, and all I could think about was his handsome face.

"Double crap!"

Chapter Nine

Luckily, Boone and the cat behaved and didn't rip apart the laundry room. They looked pleased to see me and I opened the door to let them outside. Boone ran out to find a place to pee, but the cat wanted no part of freedom. He smelled the air, then turned tail and strolled haughtily into the kitchen.

After Boone returned, I fed them, cleaned up for bed, and put on pajamas. Returning to the great room, I decided it was time to tackle the cat's matted fur and attempt to remove the burs. Surprisingly, the cat sat on my lap and allowed me to work on his mangled coat. He was patient, so I was able to take my time and make the procedure as painless as possible—for both of us. When I finished, the cat was quite beautiful. He still had some bald patches, but those would grow back in time.

Tomorrow morning, I'd call the local vet to make an appointment for him. I hadn't noticed any fleas, but I could have missed some as I was no animal expert. The cat jumped down and snuggled next to Boone on the sofa. Seeing them getting along so well made me feel good inside. *Why can't people be this accepting of others?*

. . .

WHEN I AWOKE THE FOLLOWING DAY, BOTH ANIMALS WERE ASLEEP ON MY legs, and it took me a few moments to wake my numb limbs. Boone and the cat grumbled at the interruption, but I slipped out of bed and headed to the bathroom. After getting ready for my day and returning to the bedroom, they were both gone. When I reached the living room, Boone jumped up and down, desperate to go outside.

"You got it, my man. But don't you dare run off again, or I'll have your hide." I smiled as he barked in denial at my words and bounded out the door in a dead run. The cat was by my side but still refused to leave the house. Instead, he walked over to the litter pan and took care of business.

"Oh, yeah—I have to clean that thing, don't I?" I found a covered pail and lined it with a kitchen garbage bag. There had been a scooper in the litter pan when I retrieved it from the barn, so I fished around, picked up the disgusting piles, dumped them into the pail, and quickly closed the lid.

"Well, that was disgusting." The cat wasn't offended by my comment and rubbed his body around my legs.

After letting the dog in, I fed them both and retrieved the phone number of the local veterinarian. I was in luck. They could get the cat in today as they had a cancellation. But how would I transport him? I didn't have a carrier. There had to be a box somewhere around here. Sure enough, I found a small one in the garage. When I brought it into the house, the cat jumped in and played boisterously like a kitten.

There was just enough time for a quick breakfast, then I'd pile the animals into the car. Boone wasn't an issue, and he climbed in quickly, opting for the rear seat. While the cat played in the box, I quickly closed the lid and carried him to the car's back seat. He seemed fine for a minute, and then he howled in earnest. I slid in beside him, closed the car door, and carefully opened the top. He looked petrified.

"I'm sorry, buddy, but I must take you to the vet." Before I could say anything, the cat crashed through the lid but quietly walked inside the vehicle. Once he'd seen everything, he returned to the back seat and calmly laid down next to Boone.

"That's weird. Okay, I hope you won't turn into Wile E. Coyote once I start driving."

Returning to the front, I gingerly started the engine and glanced into the rearview mirror. The cat didn't budge an inch. I was about to reverse the vehicle and remembered my promise. Quickly reciting the prayer, I backed out of the garage, drove down the driveway, and onto the road. The feline slept during the entire ride. He even waited patiently for me to open the door when we arrived at our destination. Reaching for him, he curled his body against me, purred, and wrapped his paws around my neck as I carried him inside the office, with Boone following on my heels.

At the vet, the two animals were charming. They loved the staff and stayed on their best behavior. Luckily, they could also examine Boone, so I wouldn't have to return for his previously scheduled appointment in a couple of days. Also, I gave the assistant the only vet records I had, so they wouldn't have to repeat his earlier bloodwork.

Both animals checked out fine and were given their vaccines. Neither one had any signs of ticks or fleas, but they gave me prevention for both of them, anyway. I was also notified that the cat had already been neutered. While I checked out, I spotted a plethora of cat toys on display, so I selected several of them and added them to my bill. The vet gave me feeding and care instructions for both animals, and I also purchased more food for Boone. They asked me the cat's name for his file, but I couldn't answer and said I'd call them once I selected one.

When I left the vet's office and returned the animals to the car, Gus appeared. "Just what I need," I muttered under my breath.

"Hello, Gus," I said with feigned joy. There's no way I was going to ask him anything. *So why give him fodder to spew insults at me?*

"Hmph," he growled, but I smiled at him and climbed into my car. I refused to look back at the ornery octogenarian because I knew it would make him crazy. He was probably waiting to give me a crude sneer or an insufferable middle-finger salute.

Driving away, I continued to smile. "I'll win you over one way or another, you old coot."

After returning to the cottage, the three of us spent the day together. I even persuaded the cat to join Boone and me for a walk. He stayed glued to our side and was a perfect gentleman. Boone would dash off but wouldn't go far, and I was grateful. I worked hard to make him stay nearby, although I didn't know what I was doing. But Boone seemed to understand, and that's all that mattered.

A chipmunk grabbed the cat's attention and he almost ran off. "Cat! Get back here! Geez, I have to give you a name. Cat just doesn't work for me." He returned quickly, sat down at my feet, and delicately washed his paws—extra toes and all.

I crouched down and scratched his head. "I love that extra thingamajig on each of your front feet. Hey, that's it! I'll call you Jig." He sneered at me with arrogance, pinned his ears momentarily, then stared at me as if thinking about his new moniker. "Come on, my friend. It's a cool name."

After a couple of moments, his ears came forward, the good one and what was left of the other, and then purred and rubbed against my ankles.

"I take it that 'Jig' will work for you?" He meowed sweetly, and I took that response as a yes.

"Awesome! Let's go back and get a bite to eat." I spotted Cade's truck in my driveway as we neared the cottage. He climbed out of his vehicle and waved in my direction. A red ballcap was perched on his head, and he wore a tight black and orange striped t-shirt and well-worn blue jeans. He looked positively delicious. I was about to yell a greeting when Boone took off ahead of me and ran straight for Cade, barking viciously and snapping at Cade's legs.

"What the…" Cade scrambled back into his truck and slammed the door. Unfortunately, Boone still growled at the vehicle door and I had to pull him away. "What's gotten into him?" Cade asked as he stuck his head out of the open truck window.

"I honestly don't know." Boone was still hostile and I reprimanded him and told him to sit. He finally calmed down and obeyed my command but kept a level glare on the truck. Cade pulled his head back inside, but his red cap caught the top of the window frame and dropped on the ground outside the vehicle.

Boone instantly and aggressively grabbed the cap and began ripping it to shreds, growling and spitting in the process. Then, when he was done with razing the poor hat, he peed on it.

Cade and I looked at each other, and he said, "I think we know what set him off. Wasn't I wearing that cap the first time he took after me?"

"I believe you were. Are you thinking what I'm thinking?"

"That someone must have abused him, and whoever it was, wore a red ball cap?"

"Oh my," I replied in shock. "As a matter of fact, when I rescued the poor dog, the man that had kicked Boone had worn a red ballcap. I didn't make the connection until now." Picking up the hat, I carried it to the garbage can and threw it away. "Sorry, Cade."

"No worries. I'm going to try and get out of the truck again. First, let's make sure our reasoning is sound, shall we?"

I nodded and waited as Boone watched Cade exit the vehicle. After he stepped out, Boone's tail started wagging and the dog was thrilled to see him. Cade knelt and petted Boone. "Sorry, pal. I had no idea, and I promise never to wear a red hat again. Deal?"

"Arf!"

"I guess he agrees," I replied. "Now, as Stanley would say, what can I do ya for?"

"I wanted to let you know that the fencing will be in early tomorrow morning, so if it works for you, I'll start installation around ten?"

"Sounds great," I said.

Cade looked at the house and asked, "Uh, you have company."

"What?" I turned to see what he was talking about and saw Jig waiting to go inside the cottage. "Yes, that's Boone's new cat—the one I told you about last night. His name is Jig."

"Hmm. Jig, huh? I like it—it fits him. Is he friendly?"

"Yes. But there are no guarantees—maybe he hates prison-striped t-shirts." I pointed to Cade's shirt and he hooted with a sarcastic chortle.

"Very funny, Miss Fancy Pants." He was referring to my pink and purple polka-dotted capris. They weren't very attractive, but I hadn't gotten around to buying more clothes since I arrived in town.

"Touché," I replied, then turned to walk toward the door. I glanced back at him and said, "Are you coming?"

He looked slightly startled, then answered, "Sure…you bet!" He trotted forward to catch up with me and we entered the cottage. Jig welcomed Cade with a rub around his calves and we sighed in relief.

Cade stayed with us the entire afternoon and even joined us for dinner. I still had the casserole from yesterday, which turned out to be quite tasty. We topped off the meal with vanilla-caramel ice cream but had to share it with Boone and Jig.

Cade helped with kitchen duty, and he handed me the plates to load the dishwasher. There was a loud cracking sound as Cade accidentally dropped a dinner plate onto the counter. I felt my body drop to the floor, and everything faded to black.

"YOU IDIOT! YOU'LL PAY FOR LEAVING THE KITCHEN IN SUCH A MESS, YOU filthy, incompetent pig!" Trace slams our expensive china plate on the counter. I'm struck in the face again with Trace's fist, and the force shoves me back against the unforgiving marble countertop. He grabs my arm and tosses me like a ragdoll across the kitchen table and over to the other side. My body hits the floor hard and my head bounces off the expensive porcelain tile. Blacking out for a few moments, I finally come to and grab my head, trying to ease the painful throbbing across my skull. There's a ringing in my ears as I try to think, but my mind won't focus. As I'm struggling to get my brain to work, I see a pair of expensive men's loafers in front of me, and one lifts and begins kicking me repeatedly in the stomach. I can't take it anymore—please stop, please! No more...

"HANNAH! OH, MY LORD IN HEAVEN. HANNAH, PLEASE, HONEY, HEAR MY voice and return to me. It's me, baby, it's Cade." As I tried to focus, I noticed I was huddled on the floor by the kitchen cabinets, and Cade's arms were around me, cuddling me to his chest. My body trembled and I couldn't seem to make it stop. "Hannah, can you hear me?"

"Cade, I hear you. I'm...so...sorry. I'm okay now, but please give me a few minutes to...." No words came to mind. There wasn't any way I could tell him about Trace or what had happened before I ran. I couldn't trust him or anyone because my life depended on it. But I allowed myself to stay in his arms until the shaking ceased. Then, moving away, I carefully stood up, taking advantage of the cabinets to remain upright. Cade still gently held my arm, perhaps wondering if I'd end up on the floor again.

"I'm fine…really," I said weakly. Grabbing a glass from the counter, I filled it with cold water and took a long swig with a trembling hand. When I turned to look at him, I saw compassion and understanding in his dark eyes.

"Do you want to tell me about it?" he asked kindly.

"Thank you, but no. It's nothing and I'm fine. You should probably go —I'm not very good company now and prefer to turn in for the night."

"Hannah, you had a flashback. Do you think I don't know what you just went through? I used to get them too, but luckily I now have a better handle on them. It took a lot of therapy to get where I am now. Trust me—I know those things can really kick your butt."

I looked into his eyes again and felt an instant bond. He did understand. Smiling up at him, I placed a hand on the side of his face. "You do know, don't you?"

He returned the smile and pulled me to him, holding me close. I knew this kind man was giving me the time to collect myself as I attempted to hide the horrific memory in a vault within the recesses of my fractured mind.

"Yes," he whispered into my ear and gently kissed my cheek.

Cade stayed with me for another hour until I finally shooed him out the door and told him to go home. But he turned around and pulled me close, then kissed me passionately. I knew I shouldn't have let him, but I needed his warmth and support.

We were breathing hard when he backed away, and he caressed my cheek once more and said, "Call me if you need me, got it?"

I nodded and said I'd see him in the morning.

The animals and I sat on the sofa to watch television because I still needed to unwind. I was afraid to go to bed yet, fearful of another dreaded nightmare. Both Boone and Jig fought for room on my lap, but since Boone was bigger, he won. So, my new kitty climbed onto my shoulders and fell asleep with his head buried in my neck. I never knew a cat could be this affectionate and it made me smile.

Tamara Maudelle

Upon Cade's suggestion, I streamed a couple of John Wayne movies and Cade was correct: although they were old films, they were fun to watch, and I found the characters and plotline enjoyable. When the movies were over, the three of us went to bed. Luckily, I only dreamt of Cade's handsome face, which made me grin from ear to ear while I slept.

Chapter Ten

I woke early and eagerly anticipated seeing Cade today. After I showered, I confined my hair into a French braid and carefully applied a light spackle of makeup. Donning a pair of snug white shorts, a hot pink tank top, and tennis shoes, the three of us ran downstairs and I let Boone out and cleaned the litter pan. *Yuck!* We had breakfast and I tidied up the house. I didn't want Cade to think I was a slob.

Precisely at ten, his truck drove up with a large trailer in tow. Boone and I ran out to greet him. *Man, I loved looking at this man.* Today he wore a muscle-hugging white t-shirt and stained but clean work pants. I was relieved when I noted he wore a blue cap with "Navy" written across the front. When Boone approached him, Cade was wary but he didn't have to worry. The dog was back to his usual, friendly self.

"Do you need any help?" I rested my forearms along the edge of the trailer as I peered inside.

Cade sorted the items and said, "I'm good for now. I have Huey coming over to give me a hand."

"The cute boy from the computer store?"

"That's him. He helps me out from time to time. That kid loves learning new things and is good at construction—not just computers."

"That's great. I really like him. Do you need anything from me?"

"Nah. I'm good, but I'll let you know if I do, gorgeous."

I paused as I turned to go to the cottage. He surprised me with his compliment.

"Okay," was all I said.

I spent the day reviewing and editing my first two completed novels until I was sure they were as perfect as I could make them. Then I emailed the agent and hoped she still remembered me. Now it was a waiting game.

Opening a blank document, I began writing a new book. This one would be a murder mystery, and I already had most of it planned in my head.

I kept glancing out the window between writing and tending to the pets. Cade and Huey seemed to work well together. First, I saw the two teasing one another, and then I heard joyful laughter. It made me think how great a father Cade would be. *Oh, stop, you idiot. Don't even think about it.*

Cade bent over and hefted a couple of large, heavy posts, and I watched in fascination as the muscles flexed across his back, shoulders, and down his arms. His sweat made his biceps glisten in the sun, and I couldn't tear my gaze away. I had a brief image of us in a passionate embrace and immediately stopped my crazy thoughts. At that moment, he looked up at me through the window and I swore he knew exactly what I was thinking. Cade stared at me and I couldn't look away. After several moments, his expression changed, and his face lit up with a bright, flirty smile, and he saluted. I waved back and moved away from the window because, for some reason, this man made my heart race and my body tingle.

Plopping back down in my desk chair, my brow furrowed in frustration. "What are you thinking, Serena? Or should I say, Hannah? Don't forget you're still married and can't act upon any feelings you may have for Cade. You'll have to tell him again that nothing can happen between us," I mumbled.

I felt miserable when I returned to my writing, and my creative mood had disappeared. Boone laid at my feet and appeared mournful, and I knew we both needed a long walk.

"Come on, baby. Let's take a hike through the woods. We'll also need to give the guys a bite to eat and some refreshing iced tea." Jig, who'd been lying across the middle of my desk, picked up his head and knew what I'd said. The two animals followed on my heels down to the main floor.

Opening the side door, I yelled out to the guys and asked if they'd like some lunch after I walked Boone. They replied with a resounding, "yes!" Boone ran out, sniffing until he finally found the perfect spot to pee. Exiting the door, I strolled over to the men as they were now marking where each fence post would be installed.

"Uh, guys. I forgot to mention, this is Boone's bathroom, so you'd better be careful where you step."

They both responded simultaneously in disgusted voices, "We know!"

I couldn't help myself and laughed boisterously. "I'm so sorry…." But I still giggled at the situation.

"Sure, you are, Hannah. We can tell by your laughter." Cade said and winked at me with a smile.

"After I take Boone for a walk, I'll prepare your lunch and make a large pitcher of sweet iced tea to quench your thirst."

Huey smiled widely and said, "That sounds so rad!"

After our stroll, I heard a loud engine whine as I neared the cottage. When I emerged from the woods into the yard, Cade and Huey had a firm grip on each side of a two-person gas-powered auger as it dug deep into the ground for each fence post. The machine ground and bounced until Cade decided the hole was at the required depth. They pulled out the auger, and Cade stopped the motor and moved on to the next marked spot. He started it again, and he and Huey began guiding the auger again. I watched in fascination as Cade's muscles flexed and bulged as he held tight to the machine. Even Huey held his own as the auger gyrated and bounced as it dug through the ground.

I jumped when I heard a loud scraping sound and the auger wiggled and jerked wildly. The two men tried to hang on as the machine heaved and bucked, but the jarring motion sent the two men bouncing like rag dolls back and forth, then around the hole like a carnival ride. Finally, Huey let go and was thrown off into the grass. But Cade hung on for dear life. He was now being thrashed around the hole as well as up and down, then he was spun around once more.

After the shock of seeing what was happening, I now giggled with fits of laughter. Cade still hung on for dear life, trying to use his brute strength to get the wretched machine under control.

"Cade, let go!" Huey yelled while sitting on the ground. He also chuckled and guffawed with hysterical laughter.

But Cade still hung on. Boone ran over and chased Cade around the hole while yapping at the man and machine. It was as if the dog was egging each one on and trying to gauge the winner of the fight.

I laughed so hard I could no longer stand upright. Dropping to my knees, I couldn't control my gales of glee, and my eyes watered from boisterous snortles and gibbers. It felt like my sides were splitting, and I couldn't breathe.

Cade still bobbed, bounced, and bucked like a well-trained buckaroo.

"Cade—let—go!" Huey screamed once more between his roaring cackles.

The man on the machine still writhed, jerked, heaved, and whipped, and Boone continued chasing the crazy male who refused to let the hole-digging monster win this war. But all of a sudden, the machine backfired then all was silent. Cade finally released his deadly grip and backed away, still staggering and reeling from his wild ride with the bronc. He finally collapsed on his butt and sat there, obviously a bit dizzy, but he had a massive grin of triumph on his dirt-covered handsome face.

Finally catching my breath after my hysterical laughter, I stood up and walked over to Cade. "You rode him well, cowboy. Yee-haw!" I threw my fist into the air in triumph.

He grinned up at me and said in a southern drawl, "Yes, sirree. I sho-nuff did. That stinkin' bronc won't get the best of me ever again." Cade stood, and after he wobbled a bit on his feet, I grabbed his arm to steady him.

Huey joined us, and I said, "I think you two deserve a break. Come inside, get cleaned up, and I'll make that lunch I promised you."

"Thanks, little lady. We'll take you up on your kind offer, pilgrim." Cade swaggered toward the door imitating John Wayne, but then he stumbled briefly, as the dizziness hadn't dissipated. Huey and I giggled once more, and Boone barked at Cade's heels.

After the guys cleaned up, we sat at the table and enjoyed our lunch. Of course, Boone and Jig also received a few bites of turkey that seemed to accidentally fall from everyone's plate to the floor.

After lunch, the guys returned outside to tackle the post hole digging once more. Luckily, there weren't any more mishaps with the auger, and Cade and Huey finished installing the posts. The sun was getting low in the sky and the two men said they had to take their leave. They both left with a friendly wave and I was sad to see them go. But I knew they'd return to complete the fence in the morning.

After their departure, it was time to take Boone for another walk. Jig refused to go outside again, and he returned to the living room and attacked his catnip mouse with vigor and determination to show it who was in charge.

Boone and I decided to venture farther than usual. The trails were harder to follow, but we traveled on.

"Yoohoo! Hannah!" A female voice hollered, and Boone barked with glee and took off to greet our visitor.

"Lois, it's great to see you," I replied. She quickly headed my way as Boone jogged along beside her. She gave me a loving hug, and I returned it with a happy surprise.

"My dear, you look positively radiant. But then, you're a very stunning young woman. How have you been?"

"Thank you, Lois. You're very kind. I'm well; how are you?"

"Happier than a pig in mud. Since you're here, may I take you to my favorite spot?"

"Lead the way."

Lois led Boone and me to a small, private beach area where there was a giant piece of driftwood lying on its side, parallel to the water. We sat down together, and Boone waded into the lake to quench his thirst. Sitting there for several minutes and not saying a word, we savored the sights and smells of the gorgeous landscape. The sun's rays warmed my skin and the scent of pine wafted around me. I sighed with pleasure.

Lois finally spoke up, "This has always been my favorite spot and now I hope it's yours."

"Thanks, Lois. Although I'm not sure I'd find it again."

"Trust me, Hannah, you'll always find your way here—and Boone will too. I hear you've met Cade. What do you think of him?"

"Well…"

"Come on, 'fess up, honey! You know he's a handsome hunk and a mighty fine catch. He's not one you'd want to slip off your fishing pole."

I giggled at her comment. "I know. Lois, it's not that I don't like him— I'm just not looking for a relationship. Not with any man."

Lois said nothing for a moment while staring at the lake. A smile crossed her lips as Boone chased some minnows that darted back and forth in the shallow water.

"Hmm." Her response was quiet yet pensive. After a few more minutes, she said, "I understand. But don't ever close your heart, my dear. Our time on this earth is fleeting, and you never want to miss out on what God has in store for you. The Lord above opens many doors for us, and we must remain vigilant and not lose sight of these blessings."

"Lois, I'm sorry. But I don't believe in God—not anymore." I said this quietly and hoped I hadn't hurt her feelings.

She turned to look at me, and her intense brown-eyed gaze held my attention. "I know you believe that, but there will come a time when your heart will shift and open again. God still believes in you, and He will continue to knock, pick, and poke at that wall you've built around yourself. The Lord's very patient and persistent."

Lois gently squeezed my hand, then bent down to pick up a small stick to throw for Boone. The dog yapped in joy and raced in fervor to retrieve the object. He diligently returned, dropped it at our feet in the sand, and waited for us to toss it again.

I picked up the stick and gave it a heave, and he took off as fast as his little legs could carry him. We both laughed at his antics. Boone's hip was healed, and I smiled joyfully that he could run and play like a normal, healthy dog.

"Lois, I find what you're saying hard to believe, but I'll keep an open mind."

"That's all I ask, Hannah. I know you've been terribly hurt by those you thought you could trust. But if you give your pain and fear to God, you'll be surprised at how freeing it can be. Just give it a thought, my dear.

Don't let those people in your past destroy your future—you're giving them way too much power over you, and it's time to let it go. You have so much to offer others, as well as for God's creatures." She stopped talking momentarily, then said, "Oh my, it's getting late, and the sun will be setting soon. I'm sure Jig's getting hungry and that kitty still needs to put on more weight." Standing up, she grabbed my hand and pulled me upright too. I smiled at her and called Boone back so we could return to the trails.

"Thanks, Lois. I enjoyed our conversation, and it gives me something to think about. But how did you know about my past?" We continued hiking through the woods, and she guided me toward the main path that led to my cottage.

"As you may have surmised, I'm of Native American heritage, and I'm Chippewa, or should I say Ojibwe. I come from a long line of shamans with what you'd call the sight. When we converted to Christianity, we're now considered seers or visionaries."

"So, you can visualize things that others can't?" I asked with surprise, trying not to sound skeptical.

"I know you find it hard to believe, but sometimes I do. Even as a child, I'd know things. Trust me when I say it was terrifying until my grandmother helped me understand my gift." She stopped and turned, then hugged me. "I think you know this is where you return to your cottage. It's time for me to take my leave. Goodnight, my dear, and give Jig a hug for me."

I looked at her quizzically, then said, "Goodnight, Lois. I hope I'll see you soon."

"You will, my dear. I promise." She had only walked a few feet away, but I could no longer see her. *How on earth did she move so fast?*

As Boone and I cleared the woods and entered the house, Jig ran up to us and meowed with happiness at our arrival. He purred and rubbed against each of us.

My eyes widened as I remembered what Lois said, "I'm sure Jig is getting hungry." How on earth did she know about Jig? I never mentioned him to her. How weird. Was she really psychic? *Nah!*

Chapter Eleven

The next morning, Cade and Huey arrived bright and early, and I was glad to see them. Even Boone and Jig were excited. I walked out to the side yard and greeted them with a happy smile.

"Hi, you two! It's only seven-thirty and you're already here?"

Cade grinned and sent me an enthusiastic wink. "You bet. The early bird gets the worm and all that."

Huey played with Boone, throwing the dog's tennis ball every time Boone returned it.

"Hi, Hannah! Yep, and we're hoping it won't be another bronc-riding rodeo! Right, Cade?"

"Come on, pilgrim, you're taking all the fun out of the job!" Cade responded, using a terrible imitation of John Wayne again.

Giggling with glee, I said, "I agree with Huey. We were both howling so hard with laughter we almost needed CPR." Cade gave me a goofy, cross-eyed look that made me laugh again.

"Okay, you two. Boone and I have to run to town this morning. We're going to the vet so Boone can be snipped." Cade and Huey looked at each other with painful grimaces and acted as if they wanted to protect their nether regions.

"Poor Boone! You have my sympathies, boy." Cade replied as he bent down and scratched the dog's head. Boone licked Cade's hand and Huey moved over to hug the poor mutt. Boone pinned his ears to his head and knew something was up.

With hands on my hips, I hollered, "Guys, stop it! You're upsetting him, and I don't want him to know what's going to happen. *Geez!*"

They apologized, and Cade again threw the ball for Boone to retrieve. My dog's grin returned and I sighed in relief.

"Boone, let's go!" He looked up and ran over to me. I happily picked him up and turned back to the guys. "I shouldn't be too long and I'll bring you back some breakfast."

Huey and Cade gave each other a high-five and returned to work.

When I dropped Boone off at the veterinarian, I hugged him and walked out of the office with a tear of worry in my eye. I loved that mangy mutt and didn't want anything to happen to my new best friend.

Strolling into the deli, I waited in line to place my order. The television along one side of the restaurant broadcasted the national news.

"Trace St. John, who was previously reported missing, has been found dead in Nevada. His brother Cameron would like to thank everyone involved in finding his loving brother. Trace's body and crashed vehicle were found at the bottom of the bluffs. The funeral details will be forthcoming as soon as the arrangements have been completed." The news station showed an older photo of Trace.

"There is more sad news regarding the St. John family. Trace's wife, Serena, has also been found. Unfortunately, like her poor husband, it wasn't a rescue but a recovery. Her body was found at the rock quarry, and it appears she was murdered. Both suspicious deaths remain under investigation. Funeral arrangements for Serena are pending." They posted an old picture of me, and luckily it looked nothing like the new me. "It's unknown at this time if the two deaths are related, but it's highly likely."

As I stood there, I began to shake in terror and my mind couldn't focus. I could no longer hear anything except a muffled whine, and the only thought in my head was to run. Turning quickly, I sprinted out of the deli and hurried down the sidewalk toward the end of town. I spotted a bench and sat down in shock. My body continued to shudder and I struggled to slow my panicked breathing. There was no sense of time passing, so I had no clue how long I sat there. At least my hearing had returned, but I still couldn't focus.

I heard a grunt, and standing before me was a pair of legs wearing faded jeans leading down to stained, worn sneakers. Ignoring this intruder, I still sat there, trying to stop the constant shaking and trembling. At that moment, it dawned on me that I was slowly rocking in my seat, instinctively trying to calm myself.

The pair of legs walked away and I hiccupped in my misery. But several minutes later, they returned. Hot coffee was thrust under my nose, and I thought I heard another grunt. I still ignored it. The legs moved and I felt the bench jiggle, and whoever it was now sat next to me. The coffee again appeared in front of my face, but then it was pushed into one of my hands, and the person wrapped my fingers around it. I still didn't respond. "Legs" lifted my hand that now held the coffee and guided it to my lips.

"Drink. It'll help." It was a gruff voice and it was insistent. This person still guided my shaking hand and helped me to drink the hot, whisky-ladened coffee. "That's it, now keep drinking. It'll help, girlie."

I stopped rocking and continued to drink the laced coffee. The trembling subsided. My hand was steadier now, and I could hold the drink without incident. After taking several deep breaths, I raised my head and turned to my rescuer. It was Gus.

My eyes filled with tears and I leaned against him and cried. He wrapped his arm around me and awkwardly patted my shoulder. Neither of us said a word. I could smell a note of spicy aftershave and a hint of pipe tobacco, which was comforting and, for some reason, made me feel safe.

After several moments, I sat back and Gus kindly passed me a clean handkerchief.

"Thank you, Gus."

"Hmm," he answered while handing me a sweet glazed doughnut.

I smiled to myself and thanked him again. He grumbled, "I knew it was a dinkum good idea," and quietly walked away. Watching him leave, I realized there was a kind man under that grizzled, grumpy exterior. As I gazed at his departure, I noted he'd probably been a real looker when he was younger—tall, slim, with a strong face and intelligent gray eyes. But time had not been kind to him as he now walked with a slow, arthritic gait and had very little hair left on the top of his head. But the burden he carried now was anger and resentment. Something terrible must have given this old man such a sour attitude. I shook my head, wondering what could have possibly changed this man's life so drastically.

Still shaking my head in sadness for the old guy, I stood and carried the coffee and doughnut back to my car. I sat for a while, thinking about the television broadcast.

Did everyone really think I was dead? Was I now safe from that corrupt family? Could it be true that Trace was dead, or could he and his family have been up to something? If Trace was gone, it would put Cameron in charge of the crime family. Would Cameron want revenge if he thought I'd killed his brother? I doubt it—he hated Trace. So it was a win-win for him. Hmm. There were so many variables and I didn't know what to believe.

Glancing at myself in the rearview mirror, my face had a deathly pallor, and my eyes were swollen and red-rimmed. "This won't do at all," I muttered to myself. Grabbing some makeup and eye drops from my purse, I tried to fix the damage. Once I looked somewhat presentable, I climbed out of the car and returned to the deli to order the breakfast I had promised the guys.

After returning to the cottage, I delivered their food. Cade glanced at me with concern and asked quietly if I was okay. I assured him I was and gave him a silly grin. He snickered at my antics but knew something had upset me and was polite enough to let it go.

When I entered the cottage, I went upstairs and pulled a combination lockbox from my closet. After punching in the required code, I pushed aside some paperwork and a couple of thumb drives and retrieved the phone from Kogi. I made the mistake of not checking it since I arrived at the cottage. Kogi promised to keep me posted if anything new developed that could impact my safety. After turning on the cell, several text notifications popped up, waiting to be read.

Kogi told me that both Trace and I had been pronounced dead. But what alarmed me the most was Cameron had hired several private investigators. *Was he looking for me? And if so, why?* I quickly texted Kogi and apologized for not responding, and I had received his updates and warnings.

Kogi instantly replied, "No one knows why he hired these investigators. You'll be the first to know if I find out anything new. Stay safe, Hannah."

I spent the afternoon writing as well as worrying about Boone. But I received a call that he was recovering beautifully and I could pick him up before five.

Cade and Huey were assembling the fence quickly, and they would finish up tomorrow. The vinyl picket fence panels matched the color of the house and I had asked for three gates, one along each side of the fence and one at the rear.

I invited the men to dinner and said we would eat after I retrieved Boone from the vet's office. They gladly agreed. A prepared chicken and biscuit casserole sat warming in the oven. The guys said they'd come in and clean up, then be ready for dinner when Boone and I returned. Huey offered to prepare a salad and Cade would set the table. I gladly accepted.

When I arrived at the office, Boone wagged his tail with glee, and Dr. Neumann said he was doing well. After paying the bill, she handed me the cone of shame and said Boone must wear it for a week until the incision healed. I could only remove it when he had his meals or for a bath.

The vet showed me how to take the offending thing on and off, and Boone was none too happy. He hit the side of the exit door frame on the way out and turned to give me a glaring stare.

"Sorry, bub." I patted his behind and he followed me out to the car. After carefully guiding him into the back seat, he sat down and wagged his tail again, obviously thrilled to be going home.

After pulling into the cottage's driveway, I helped him out of the car and into the house. He still kept bumping into everything, but Dr. Neumann said he'd quickly acclimate to the atrocious e-collar.

"Boone! You look handsome, my friend. But I'm sorry about the lampshade, dude!" Cade said and knelt to hug the dog. Boone gloried in the attention and Huey joined Cade on the kitchen floor. My sweet puppy laid down and rolled onto his back, relishing their yummy belly rubs. The cone scraped and ground against the tiled floor, but no one cared.

"Just let me wash up and dinner will be ready," I said, but everything was already on the table. "Oh my, you two have been busy."

"Yep! We didn't want you to have to worry about it," Huey replied, his freckles brighter than usual on his handsome, youthful face.

"Let's eat," Cade replied. After washing my hands, he held my chair, and I sat happily down. Jig showed up, and of course, all of us dropped meat now and again on the floor, which drove Boone crazy. He couldn't grab any of the chicken that hit the tile due to the cone of shame. Cade asked me if he could slip him a couple of pieces, and I said I didn't mind. The food was delicious and the company even better. After the meal, the men offered to help with the dishes and I accepted. I fed both Boone and Jig and now their tummies were also happy. Boone tried to evade the wretched cone, but he finally sat down and let me reattach it to his collar.

We heard a honk in the driveway and Huey said it was his ride. He and his friends were going to a movie and would see us tomorrow. After wishing him fun and a quick goodbye, I flipped on the lights.

"It's awfully dark all of a sudden." As soon as the words were out of my mouth, I saw a bright flash of light and heard a large *boom*.

"You'll be experiencing one of our famous thunderstorms. It's why we called this place Storm Harbor. The summer deluges are a sight to behold. So hang on to your socks." He saw the strange look on my face and asked, "You're not afraid of thunderstorms, are you?"

"Uh, no. But I had no idea the name actually meant something. I hope Boone and Jig aren't afraid of them. What about you, Cade? You were a veteran on active duty in the Middle East."

"You'd think it would be a problem for me, but for some reason, it isn't. But fireworks are another story. I'm not too fond of them." Cade visibly shuddered as he closed the dishwasher. "Okay, we're done here, and I should get going before it starts raining cats and dogs."

"Do you have to leave?" I almost kicked myself for my sudden whiney request, but Cade smiled, hooked his arm into mine, and guided me to the living room.

"I can stay a little while and we can watch the storm together." There was another brilliant flash and a thunderous boom. It made me jump, but I found it exhilarating. I looked for Boone and Jig but only spotted the cat. Walking to the laundry room, I found the dog waiting to go outside.

"Okay, bub, but you better make it fast before the rain starts." He darted outside and did his business, then returned quickly as the rain poured in earnest.

There were several more flashes and loud, ferocious cracks. I jumped in surprise and Boone looked at me in fear. "Isn't that cool, Boone? I love it!" I said, keeping an even and confident tone. Boone decided it was safe and followed on my heels back to the sofa to join Cade. "Should I light a few candles in case the lights go out?"

"You don't have to. An on-demand generator is installed outside, and it'll kick on within a few seconds if the power goes out."

"Cool! It seems you thought of everything when you fixed up this place." I grinned at him and kissed his cheek. My face blushed with embarrassment and Cade smiled kindly.

The storm was now in full force, and as Cade had said, it was a doozy. Jig and Boone settled down next to us on the sofa that faced the large windows overlooking the lake. The animals appeared only a little nervous by the violent noise. Cade and I smiled in delight at the ferocity of the storm. Of course, we also jumped several times as the lightning viciously attacked the raging Great Lake and everything surrounding it. Several more lightning strikes flashed and boomed and the lights flickered and went out. After a few moments, the generator kicked on. The noise and light display of the storm lasted for another ten minutes, causing the windows to shudder from the intensity of the strikes until the storm finally moved away.

"Wow!" was all I said.

"I know, right? I wouldn't recommend a storm hater to move into this area of the lake, that's for sure." As I smiled back at him, he moved closer and pulled me to him for a passionate kiss. It took me by surprise, just like that crazy storm. Moaning in response, Cade deepened the kiss and then laid me back on the sofa. Jig yowled in warning. We quickly sat back up and made sure the cat was okay—which he was. He was simply indignant. The cat jumped to the floor and stalked off in a huff, found his catnip mouse, and tossed it into the air. Boone moved away, too, settling down to munch on his favorite pig toy.

"That sure took the wind out of my sails. I thought we killed the poor animal," Cade said. Now frustrated, he ran his hand through his hair and got up to walk it off.

"He's fine. Only a bit miffed," I replied. Boone jumped up next to me again, along with his pig, and Cade also sat back down and started another conversation.

"Are you okay, Hannah? I know you were upset when you returned from town this morning."

"It's nothing I'd like to talk about now, Cade. I hope you understand."

"Not a problem. But if you ever need to talk, I'm told I'm a good listener."

"Thanks. I'll be sure to remember that. One thing, though—I saw Gus's good side today. He was kind to me and I found it refreshing and surprising."

"See! I told ya—he doesn't show it often, but it's definitely there. From the rumors I've heard, he was in love for years with a woman who lived around here but never told her so, and then she died suddenly. He's bitter about it and that's why he acts the way he does. Apparently, he can't forgive himself for never admitting his love for her."

"That poor man. I guess I'd feel that way too."

"Don't ever let him know you feel sorry for him—he'll probably spit in your eye and kick you in the shins," Cade chuckled and squeezed my hand.

"Trust me, I won't."

"It's getting late, my sweet. I'd better go." He leaned in and kissed me again. What surprised me was I wanted him to continue—and he did. We both moaned and I didn't want him to stop. I shifted my body, allowing him to get closer. The shrill ring of Cade's phone jerked us apart.

Cade swore and apologized for the interruption. He stood up to answer the phone and walked to the kitchen to continue the conversation with whoever was on the other end of the line. It wasn't long before he returned after disconnecting the call.

"That was my mom. She and the entire family would like to invite you to dinner on Saturday. Their home is only an hour from here, and I'd love for you to meet them."

"Cade, I don't know. We don't know each other well and I'm not sure…."

"Hannah, you'll love my family. They're kind and love everyone, plus my mom's an excellent cook. She's the typical Italian mother and her grandmother's lasagna recipe is…." Cade put his fingers to his mouth and kissed them in the typical Italian fashion and continued with a *"delizioso."*

"If you're sure they don't mind, Cade."

"I'm positive. How about I pick you up around two in the afternoon?"

I nodded in agreement and then followed him to the door.

"It's a date then," he replied and gave me a quick kiss. He was about to take a step onto the wet pavement on the porch but turned around and took my hand. Turning it over so it was palm up, he raised it to his lips and gently kissed my sensitive skin.

Raising his eyes to mine, he simply stared at me and said, "Sweet dreams, my lovely Hannah." Turning quickly, he hopped off the porch and departed in his big red truck.

After closing the door, I released a heavy sigh. Every time Cade and I were together, I felt our bond strengthen. I couldn't help but think I was making a grave mistake by pursuing our relationship. Would he eventually hurt me or would I be the one who would ruin this good thing? Was there a future for us because running was all I'd ever known? Would fear, danger, and self-doubt continue to be my constant companion? I didn't know.

Chapter Twelve

The following day the power was back on, so Cade and Huey were able to finish the fence. It took most of the day and it looked wonderful. Boone seemed to like it and had to inspect it from one end to the other. Surprisingly, Jig also came out and seemed pleased with the results. I concluded that the cat felt safe inside the fenced yard and would probably take advantage of it during clement weather.

As I surveyed the finished enclosure, I pondered what I'd like to plant inside the fence. It seemed bare and could use a few plants, shrubs, and flowers. Cade agreed with me and said Gus was a retired horticulturist and excellent at landscaping design.

"Cade, you've got to be kidding! He barely tolerates me, and just because he showed one act of kindness doesn't mean he'll treat me any better now."

"You'd be surprised, Hannah. He loves plants and flowers and would be tickled to be able to plan and design this area for you. Let me ask him and I'll tell you what he says."

"Well…only if you're the one to ask him. And I can't ever describe Gus as being tickled," I replied skeptically. Cade gave me a wolfish grin and I snorted in derision. This made him laugh and I couldn't help myself and joined in.

Huey returned from stowing the tools into the back of Cade's truck and threw the ball for Boone. The red-haired boy chuckled when Jig joined in on the fun, chased the ball, tackled it, then sat down, covering it with his fluffy tush. Boone barked at Jig and was unhappy that the cat stole his toy. Jig delicately licked one paw, then rolled over and let Boone steal the ball back.

We laughed at their antics, then Cade and Huey said they had to leave. I hugged them both and thanked them for their hard work. Cade gave me a flirty wink, and Huey lowered his head and muttered a quiet and embarrassed, "no problem."

After they departed, I ran into town to finally purchase a new wardrobe. My current selection of clothing left a lot to be desired, and it was time for an upgrade. There were some fashionable boutiques in town and I found everything I needed. After returning home, it started to rain, and more storms were brewing. I put my purchases away, fed the cat and dog, then myself. Sitting in front of the television that evening, I watched the news. There wasn't anything new regarding my husband, and I sighed with relief. Jig and Boone joined me on the sofa, and we watched some old reruns, and then it was time for bed.

As soon as I fell asleep, the nightmare started.

I'M FINISHING THE DISHES AND TIDYING THE HOUSE. TRACE TEXTS ME, SAYS he'll be home late, and orders me to have dinner ready by ten. This is as good a time as any. Moving toward the attic, I pull down the ladder and climb up and enter the space. I scramble to the far side, find my luggage, and toss it down to the hallway below. Descending the ladder, I return it to its folded position, grab my bag, and go downstairs. I listen intently for any sounds from outside in case Trace decides to come home earlier than expected. All is quiet.

I reach into the bag and pull out the phone Kogi gave me. After turning it on, I text his grandson, telling him tonight is the night. He responds immediately and confirms I have the address where he'll meet me with the new vehicle. I pull out my small wallet, stuff both the wallet and phone into my pockets, and grab the car keys from the kitchen.

Going into the garage, I climb into the Mercedes and stow my bag in the front seat beside me. Hitting the button above the rearview mirror, the garage door opens, and I quickly reverse and leave the house. It'll take approximately forty minutes to reach Kogi's grandson's garage. Luckily, it's dark outside, and I hope none of the neighbors will notice me leaving.

Letting out a sigh of relief, I'm now about twenty miles from the house and entering the higher elevation of the bluff area. As I continue driving, I spot a car's headlights about a mile behind me. As I go around the bluff and up around Hanover Cliffs, I can no longer keep an eagle eye on the vehicle in my rearview mirror. I see a flash of lights, and the car is now coming up rapidly behind me. Speeding as fast as these hazardous roads will allow, I try to outrun it. But the predator is still gaining on me.

Jerking the wheel, I attempt to take a side road. However, the vehicle chasing me has gained too much distance and rams my car along the rear bumper. A panicked scream escapes my lips as my vehicle skids and shudders toward the cliff's edge, and I brake frantically to stop the careen of the Mercedes. It finally halts, and I quickly exit the car, move to the other side, and crouch down. The other vehicle nears me and stops. The headlights shine directly onto my vehicle.

I hear a door open.

"Serena...I know you're there...." Trace says in his, unsufferable, arrogant voice. "You might as well come out, you stupid little piece of cow dung! I put a tracking device on your car a couple of days ago. You were spending too much time at the soup kitchen, and I figured you were up to something. What were you doing there, Serena? Hmm? And where were you headed tonight? Don't bother trying to lie to me, you filthy whore. I know you were running away, so don't deny it." I can hear crunching as he walks over to my vehicle. Learning well from Kogi, I wait and let him approach me. The only problem is, from where I'm hiding, the car is to my left, and the cliff is to my right. There's no place to run.

Standing up, I face the jerk, who I will no longer let hurt me. But I want him to think he has the upper hand and I'll do anything for him.

"Trace. I'm so sorry, but nothing is going on—I'm only doing what you asked of me. You know I volunteer because it's what you want. That's all. About tonight...I was only going for a drive. You know how confusing *things get for me; sometimes, I need fresh air. I'm sorry if I messed up again, and I'll do anything if you'll forgive me—please, Trace. Anything....*" I pretend to cry and lower my eyes just enough so he thinks I'm in submission. But I watch him through my lashes.

"*It's too late, moron. Tonight, you die, and no one will care.*"

He lunges toward me and I quickly sidestep him, spin around, then kick him hard in the solar plexus. I hear the air as it's shoved out of his lungs by my forceful attack, but I continue my assault. Punching him several times in the face, including his nose, then another hard kick to his groin lays him flat on the ground.

After a few moments, I stand there. Blood is pounding in my ears, and I move to return to my vehicle, but he grabs my foot and I lose my balance, landing hard on the unforgiving ground. He rolls over and is now on top of me.

No! I scream in my head. "Never again!" I finally yell out loud at him.

I punch him repeatedly. Some blows make their target; some don't. We're both fighting in earnest now, but he's unable to land a single fist against me. Rolling together across the ground, I finally get a solid grip on his jacket and shove him hard, just as Kogi had taught me in my lessons. One minute Trace is there; the next, he's gone. I can't see anything on this side of the car as we've rolled down a slight incline where the headlights from our vehicles can't be seen. Sitting up, I try to orient myself. My eyes widen in horror as I'm mere inches from the cliff's edge.

"*Oh, my heavens!*" *I sit there in shock, my entire body shaking with anger, fear, and adrenaline. What do I do? I scoot away from the cliff and try to stand. My legs refuse to hold me the first time and I land on my butt again. Trying again, I'm finally able to stay upright. Stumbling back up the incline, I return to the vehicles and try to think. Feeling sick, I run over to a scrubby patch of grass and throw up. I heave several times until I'm sure there can't possibly be anything left in my stomach.*

I sit there for several moments, then decide what I must do. Walking to Trace's expensive car, I climb inside and drive the car toward the slope of the cliff and stop the vehicle. I put the car into neutral and climb out of the Ferrari. For a moment, I didn't think the car would start to roll, but after a minute, it finally does. The little sports car picks up speed as gravity pulls it down, and it careens over the same cliff that took Trace's life.

I stand staring at the cliff, trying to make my mind work and decide what to do next; I finally return to my vehicle and call Kogi's grandson.

"Kyle, it's me. I'm afraid there's a change in plan. Can you come to my location?" He replies that he can and I give him directions. It seems like forever as I wait for him to arrive. I worry that at any moment, Trace will come up from the cliff and attack me again. Sitting in my vehicle with the doors locked, I keep scanning everything around me—at least, what I can see from only the car's headlights. My hands won't stop shaking.

When Kyle finally arrives, I inhale a deep breath of relief, and I can't help but hug him. He's patient and gives me time to explain what has transpired. Kyle nods in understanding but says we need to get moving. He then tells me to get into my car and follow him. After several miles, we arrive at a large, out-of-the-way gravel pit. Kyle walks to the trunk of his vehicle and pulls out a dead woman's body.

"What are you doing?!" I shriek.

"Hannah, my grandfather already explained this to you, so don't worry. A body is needed, and this woman is a close match to your looks, height, and weight. We'll place her in the driver's seat of your vehicle and set the car on fire. That should do the trick." Kyle sets the poor woman in the passenger seat, then drives the vehicle to the pit of the quarry. He moves her body into the driver's seat, then douses the car in gasoline and lights a match. Whoosh! The once beautiful Mercedes is a flaming bonfire.

I stare in horror, but Kyle guides me to his vehicle, and we drive away from the second nightmare of the evening.

Returning to his garage, he gives me instructions on the gifted vehicle. Even in shock, I'm pleasantly surprised by the car. It's a restored Oldsmobile Cutlass, and its body is painted a stunning, shiny metallic black. Even the interior seats are high-quality black leather and look brand new. He also shows me where two handguns and ammunition are hidden. I watch in curious silence as Kyle tosses buckets of dirt over the car's exterior.

He looks at my questioning expression and says, "It's better that the car doesn't draw too much attention, so this was the best thing I could *come up with without destroying the new paint job." He finishes the dusting chore with a sly smirk and brushes off his hands.*

Feeling bewildered again, Kyle makes me promise to always say the St. Michael prayer every morning before I drive the vehicle.

I use his bathroom to clean up and change into fresh clothes that came from a travel bag in the trunk of the Cutlass. After giving him a grateful hug, I leave to begin my terrifying journey. Will it be worse than the one I've already been through?

I BOLTED UPRIGHT IN BED, SCARING JIG AND BOONE. "IT'S ALRIGHT, GUYS. Just another bad dream." Now that my nightgown was soaked in sweat, I rose, changed into a dry one, and returned to bed. Luckily, no more horrible dreams plagued my sleep for the remainder of the night.

The next morning dawned bright and clear as the rain finally stopped. Today I'd be running into town to buy groceries. After taking care of the animals, I climbed into the car and went to start the engine, but it wouldn't turn over.

"Come on...please don't do this to me." I tried several more times and it refused to budge. "Dang it!" Sitting there contemplating what to do, I rubbed my eye in pain. Pulling down the visor to look into the mirror, the prayer dropped into my lap. After discovering an eyelash caused my discomfort, I removed the ornery thing and looked down at the paper staring back at me.

"Shoot. I forgot to say it, so is that the problem?" I asked no one in particular. Reciting the prayer, I tried to start the car once more. It turned over and purred like a kitten. "Hmm."

Backing out of the driveway, I drove down the tree-lined winding road. Glancing down, I turned on the stereo. When I looked up again, I screamed as a giant tree was directly in my path!

"No!" I knew I would hit it as there was no time to brake. For some reason, I don't remember much after that moment. The next thing I knew, I was several feet on the other side of the downed tree and facing the same direction I was initially headed. My hands shook and I put the car in park and sat there, trying to figure out what had happened.

On unsteady legs, I climbed from the vehicle and walked around the car, looking for any damage. It was in pristine condition, as usual. I walked back toward the massive tree in the road, bent down to look at it, then back at my car. Scratching my head, I continued looking at the car, the downed tree, and back again.

"That was a sight to behold, my dear."

I jerked around and saw Lois standing at the edge of the woods with her hands on her hips. Her face was animated with excitement and her smile filled with joy.

"Lois! What are you doing here?" I exclaimed in surprise.

"Going for my usual constitutional, Hannah. What I just witnessed was a gift from Heaven. Glory be to God above!" She crossed herself and snickered with happiness. "I was coming off the trail and saw the miracle."

"What happened, Lois? I don't remember much, just seeing the gigantic tree in the road, and then the next thing I knew, I was several feet on the other side of it."

"It was the prettiest thing I've ever seen. There was a bright shimmer around your vehicle, and your car just rose in the air and glided like magic to the other side. Then the good Lord set it gently back down onto the road. It was astounding! You certainly have an angel on your shoulder."

She came over to me and hugged me. "Hannah, you're shaking like a leaf. Come back to your car and sit. And if I were you, I'd call the sheriff and tell him about the tree. We don't want another unsuspecting driver to hit that gigantic pine."

"You're right." Lois and I climbed into the car and I grabbed my phone to dial 911. I reported the tree and its precise location. After hanging up, I sat with Lois for a few minutes, collecting my thoughts. I then told her what had transpired this morning—the car not starting and the prayer I'd promised to say each day.

"Oh my. St. Michael is powerful and one you want with you at all times. " You're blessed, indeed," Lois said, patting me on the shoulder.

"I suppose...but I don't believe in God."

"Hmm. You keep repeating that, but I have to say, I think you're actually on the fence about Him. You do believe in Him but are simply angry about your past. Trust me, child, He's still there and has always been taking care of you. God works through many people and circumstances. If you knew how many times He's protected you, it would make your head spin."

"How do you know that?" I asked in disbelief. "I've gone through so much in my life and He was never there to help me."

"When your stepfather was about to rape you, didn't someone come to the door and the interruption stopped him? How many times when you were at school did a teacher or friend tell you they were there for you and would help if you ever needed them? Why did your husband turn out to be impotent, so he could never rape you? You need to think about these instances, Hannah, and know that the good Lord above was running interference. God has been there—always. Just ponder what I've said, will you?" She squeezed my hand and gave me a bright smile.

"I will, Lois."

"Good. I'd better go, my dear. These old joints won't limber up if I don't get my walking in. I'll catch you later." Lois exited the car and disappeared back into the woods just as the sheriff arrived. He pulled off to the other side of the road and exited his vehicle.

"Howdy, ma'am," he said kindly as he approached my car. "I'm Sheriff McKenzie—but everyone calls me Mac. You must be the one who reported the downed tree. We appreciate it—it could kill somebody. That was one doozy of a storm last night and these old pines tend to take a beating. By the way, are you okay?"

"Yes, sir, I am. Thanks for asking. Lois stayed with me until you arrived."

"Lois?"

"Yes. Hmm...I don't know her last name. Nice looking tall woman in her early sixties?"

"Can't say I know the name or recognize her description." He took off his hat and scratched his head in confusion. "Oh, well. She could be visiting someone around here. You're the new owner of Storm Harbor, right? Umm, Hannah Renault?"

"That's me." I didn't like his questions but tried to appear calm and unfazed. "Do you need me for anything else, Sheriff? I'm heading to town for groceries."

"Nope. It's all good here. I have help coming, and we'll set up flares and barricades until Ben and his crew get here to remove that tree. It should only take a few hours, but I recommend you wait until then to return from town. Have a nice day, ma'am."

"Thank you, Sheriff Mac. I most certainly will." After giving him a wave, I put the car in gear. I glanced in the rearview mirror and he was scratching his head as I drove away. The poor man must have been mystified as to how my vehicle ended up on the other side of the giant downed tree that covered both lanes and the shoulders. I took one last look, and the sheriff shook his head and returned to his cruiser.

For some reason, I felt a tear in my eye and said, "Thank you. But was it really you, St. Michael?" At that moment, the engine roared then quieted down again to its usual purr. More tears gathered in my eyes and slid down my cheeks. It was then that I thought maybe, just maybe, my hardened heart against God emitted a resounding *crack*.

Chapter Thirteen

Today was Saturday, and I'd be going with Cade to have dinner with his family. I was apprehensive but excited. After caring for the pets, I perused my closet and decided to dress up for the occasion. The turquoise floral short-sleeved wrap-around dress, along with silver petite-heeled shoes and sterling silver jewelry, would work well. Using a bit more makeup than normal, I decided I was ready. Grabbing a matching handbag, I headed downstairs and waited for Cade to arrive. It wasn't long until I heard a vehicle approach, and when I glanced out the front window, an older model, cherry red Camaro sat in my driveway.

I knew I should've waited for Cade to come to the door, but I couldn't wait to see the car. Rushing out, I trotted over to him as he climbed out of the vehicle.

"Oh, Cade, it's fabulous! What's the year?"

"Why thank you, gorgeous! It's a 1970 SS. I worked hard on this baby and I'm proud to say it's finally done. It took me five years, but it was worth it."

"I'll say." I stuck my head inside the car and I could smell the leather seats. "It's absolutely cherry. Do people still say that?" I giggled and ran my hand along the side of the car. "Did you paint it too?"

"That I didn't do. I have a good friend who did that tedious job, but she does excellent work."

"She?" I asked in surprise, and maybe with a bit of jealousy.

"Uh-huh. Hannah, do I see a hint of green in those brown eyes?"

"Why do you say that?" I quickly turned away and walked back toward the cottage. "I just have to lock up. I'll be right back." Cade's chuckle could be heard as I walked away. "Men!" I complained under my breath.

Cade and I talked all the way to his parent's house. We had a lot in common, and he entertained me with his quick wit. When we arrived, I was awed by their large and lovely house. It was beautifully landscaped with stone walkways, flowering shrubs, colorful roses, and well-trimmed, mature trees.

Cade watched me biting my lip as he turned off the engine and squeezed my hand in reassurance. "Hannah, there's no need for you to be nervous. You'll love them and they'll also love you. Come on." He took my hand and led me to the front entrance.

An attractive, well-coiffed woman opened the door to greet us. She was tall, thin, dark-haired, and had fantastic hazel eyes. "Cade! How's my favorite child?" She hugged him fiercely and Cade grinned with happiness.

"Now, Mom, you call each one of us your favorite child. But thanks anyway." Cade kissed her cheek and pulled me close to his side. "Mom, I'd like you to meet Hannah. Hannah, this is my mom, Esther."

"Come here, you gorgeous thing." She pulled me close, hugged me, and kissed my cheek.

After she let me go, I said, "Thank you for your kind invitation to dinner and I'm very pleased to meet you."

"Kind, shmynde. It's nothing, and we had to see the young woman that my son has been going on about. Come in, dear. I want you to meet everyone."

She ushered me into a fantastic entryway. The ceiling was high, and a sweeping staircase led to a second level. The impressive marble floor shone brightly under the elegant yet tasteful chandelier. I could hear a commotion coming from a large adjoining room.

"Come, come." Mrs. Copano hooked her arm in mine and led me to a spacious kitchen that overlooked the back of the house. Immense windows opened onto a giant deck and an exquisite backyard.

"Uncle Cade!" Two dark-haired boys around nine years old hugged Cade. They had to be twins, but not identical. A little girl with curly blonde hair giggled with delight and ran over to Cade. He picked her up and she squealed with glee. All three children had the same expressive Italian dark brown eyes.

"Hannah, these little monsters belong to my sister and her husband." He gestured toward the twin boys and introduced us. "Julian and Josiah, I'd like you to meet Hannah."

I smiled at them and said, "I'm very pleased to meet you. You two are very handsome, indeed." They blushed slightly and timidly shook my hand. Then they ran off toward the living room.

Cade laughed and said, "And this beauty is Jennah." She smiled at me and stuck her finger in her mouth.

"Hi, Jennah. I'm pleased as punch to meet you." I winked at her and she gave me a bright, coy grin.

"I'm three." She held up three fingers with pride. She wiggled, Cade put her down, and she followed her brothers to the other room.

A stunning woman in her late twenties walked up to me. "Hi, Hannah. I'm Cade's sister, Delta, and the mother of the crazy three. It's great to finally meet you. My husband, Jay, is on the deck with Cade's brother, Phoenix. Jay is the blond man—hence Jennah's golden tresses."

"I'm pleased to meet you, Delta. I'll try remembering everyone's name, but I may need reminders."

"Not a problem, Hannah. Just ask, and we'll gladly help you," Delta politely offered.

Esther introduced me to Cade's older brother, Phoenix, and his fiancée, Rachel. Phoenix was also good-looking and was taller than Cade by at least two inches. His fiancée was a pretty, slim, petite redhead with intelligent, bright green eyes.

An older, handsome gentleman walked into the kitchen and kissed Esther. This had to be Cade's dad, Frank, and it was apparent where Cade inherited his good looks. His dad was tall with a thick head of dark, curly black hair, distinguished gray sideburns, dark brown intelligent eyes, and a square jaw with a cleft chin. Cade was the younger spitting image of his father. Frank greeted me with kindness and gave me a warm hug.

"Welcome to the Copano menagerie, Hannah. We're thrilled to meet you," Frank said in a deep and friendly tone.

I thanked him and we sat down for our meal.

The dinner tasted delicious, and as Cade had said, his mother's lasagna recipe was spectacular. I thoroughly enjoyed myself, and the entire family made me feel at home. I laughed at their jokes and it surprised me how close they were and how well they got along. This wasn't something I'd ever experienced before in a family and it touched my heart.

The men cleared the table and the women took care of the dishes. They gave me the task of loading the dishwasher, and for some reason, I enjoyed it as well. Afterward, we retired to the living room and sat on the plush furniture. The children played on the floor and were well-behaved and happy.

Esther spoke up after a few minutes. "You know, we should all attend Mass together tonight. It's been so long since we've done this and it would be fantastic if we could go together. What do you say?"

The rest of the family said it was a good idea, but Cade looked at me and then at his mother. "Mom, I don't think that'll work for us. Hannah isn't religious and I'm not even sure she's Christian, let alone Catholic. Maybe some other time."

"Oh, hogwash. Anyone can come to church. It's just one hour and it won't kill her. What do you say, Hannah? All you have to do is sit there and enjoy the music." Esther must have seen my pained expression and said, "Unless you don't want to, dear. It's okay if you'd rather not—I'm so sorry I pushed you, Hannah." Her kind words broke my heart, and I felt terrible for upsetting her.

"No! It's okay—really. My family was Christian but of no specific denomination. It's just that I'm not sure what I believe anymore." I answered sincerely, "I wouldn't mind coming along—if you'll have me."

Cade's father spoke up and said compassionately, "Only if you're sure, Hannah. We wouldn't want you to feel uncomfortable. But I agree with Esther; our church has an amazing praise band, and I think you'd enjoy it."

"Then I'd love to come." Putting a big smile on my face, I squeezed

Cade's hand. He kissed my cheek and I was now actually looking forward to it.

When it was time to drive to church, we piled into three vehicles, but my nervousness reared its ugly head. But when we arrived, everyone in the family was encouraging and the other people in the church welcomed me with open arms.

After sitting in the pew, I admired the statues, murals, and candles. The smell of incense lingered in the air, and I found it comforting. The altar drew my gaze and I studied the enormous yet tasteful crucifix. A sense of wonder went through me, yet I was a little unsure. My mother had dozens of crosses all over our house and claimed she was Jesus's avid follower, although I know now she'd been putting on a good show. After my stepfather took a sexual interest in me, she continually told me I was a child of the devil and that God hated me for being a Jezebel. I would burn in Hell for tempting her husband and causing him to sin. Tears filled my eyes and I stared down at my hands. Scrambling in my purse, I pulled out a tissue.

Cade put his arm around me. "Hannah, are you alright? There's nothing here that can hurt you, sweetheart. I promise." He took my hand, brought it to his mouth, and kissed it warmly.

"I'm sorry, Cade. It's nothing to do with you or the church. A painful memory from childhood just flashed into my mind, that's all." I didn't want to say anything more, and he didn't push it. Giving me a kind smile, he hugged me and held my hand.

"I understand," was all he responded.

The praise band began to play their instruments, and they sang joyously. I followed everyone's lead and stood up. They were correct; the music was astounding. It filled the entire church and the congregation joined in with enthusiasm.

I watched the priest and three others approach the altar. They knelt and crossed themselves before they climbed up the step. The service fascinated me, but the parishioners were most surprising. Throughout the Mass, I watched their expressions and wished I could feel what they were experiencing. So many emotions moved through them during different parts of the service, and I found it overwhelming. I saw happiness, sadness, contemplation, piety, and some even appeared regretful. *How does coming to this place make them feel this way? Is it like this for everyone who's a believer?*

I felt someone watching me and discovered Julian staring at me, one of Delta's twin boys. When I returned his gaze, he sent me a knowing expression beyond his years. It was as if he knew what I was thinking and understood my confusion and questions. He smiled back and gave me a nod.

After the service, Cade still held my hand as we walked toward the car. I spotted Julian talking with the priest, but as he stepped away, I told Cade I needed a moment to speak with the boy. Cade nodded and moved away.

I approached the young child and asked, "Julian, why did you look at me that way at the end of the service? You looked like you knew something and wanted to speak with me."

"Yeah," he said, shuffled his feet, and looked around. Then he took my hand and guided me to the flowering shrubs along the sidewalk. "When I grow up, I want to be a priest. Ever since I could walk, that's all I've ever thought about. Mom says I have the calling, and Father Conti thinks so too. When I looked at you during Mass, I heard a loud voice in my head that said, 'Tell her that her mother was wrong to turn her against me and that I love Hannah dearly. I have always been with her and will never leave her side. Deep in her heart, she knows this as well.' That's what I heard, so now I'm telling you." Julian motioned me to stoop down to his level and he kissed my cheek. Afterward, he skipped toward the car and joined his brother.

I turned away, pulled out another tissue from my purse, wiped my eyes, and blew my nose. *How could a nine-year-old know this unless someone told him? But who would have, except God? But that's crazy.*

After collecting myself, I strolled to the car and climbed in beside Cade. He kindly said nothing about my tear-stained face.

We stayed at Cade's parent's house for a couple more hours, and they all had me laughing again. While preparing to leave, I happily hugged each of Cade's family.

"I want to thank all of you for your warm welcome and hospitality. You made me feel like one of the family, and I want you to know how much this experience has meant to me." I felt tears pooling in my eyes again and my cheeks flushed warmly.

"My dear, you're welcome here any time," Esther said sincerely, and everyone else agreed. "You're one of the family, and I hope you'll visit us again very soon."

I received more hugs, and Cade and I returned to his car. We didn't say much on the hour drive home, but it was a comfortable silence. So much information was going through my mind and I wasn't sure how to process everything. And I believe Cade understood this.

When we reached home, he escorted me to my door and kissed me sweetly.

"Cade, thanks so much for inviting me to meet your family. You're a fortunate man, indeed."

"I know. Wait until you meet the rest of my relatives—it's mind-boggling!" He moved his hands over his head as if his brain was exploding. I giggled and gave him a warm hug. Cade wrapped his arms around me, and we held one another, enjoying intimacy and friendship. Reluctantly letting each other go, he moved away slightly and then kissed me once more. Before it went too far, he backed up, smiled at me, and departed.

While closing the door behind me, Jig and Boone greeted me with excitement and I knew I'd better let the dog out before he piddled on the floor.

That night, snuggled in bed with my new best friends, I reviewed the day and thought about what Julian had said. I knew the opening in the wall that I had wedged between God and me had just cracked a little wider. Even after today, I still had that niggling sense of doubt pushing at the back of my mind. *How did Julian know about my pas*t, *and would I be destined to repeat the same mistakes in the future?*

Chapter Fourteen

S unday dawned bright and clear, and I couldn't wait to spend time with Jig and Boone and take a few hours to work on my book. Cade had called, asking if it was okay that his nephew Julian had told him about the voice he'd heard about me and my past.

I stumbled over my words when I tried to respond. "Cade, I don't know what to say…it's not something I talk about. But Julian hit the nail on the head and his comments stunned me. I'm still not sure how to process it…." Trailing off, I waited for Cade to answer.

After a few tense moments, he said, "Hannah. I'm sorry if you think Julian or I are intruding into your personal life, and I sincerely apologize. It was never our intention—we only wanted to help."

"No…no. There's no need for an apology. It's just surprising, that's all."

Cade spoke again, "Julian has always had what we call 'the gift.' He's been religious since he started to talk at a year old and would seem to know things. It's bizarre, but we understand his love for God and that he's wise beyond his years. I also hope you understand Julian means well."

"I do—really. Just give me time so I can process what Julian told me. A lot is happening in my head right now—I hope you'll be patient with me, Cade."

"That's not a problem, sweetie. By the way, I spoke with Gus and he'd be happy to design the landscaping inside the fence. He was positively giddy." Cade chuckled at his comment, then said. "Well, he wasn't *exactly* giddy but pleased, and he even said it was a dinkum good idea." He laughed again and I couldn't help myself and giggled too.

Cade continued, "Anyway, Gus said he'd like to stop by on Monday around ten in the morning—if that works for you. Don't worry, I'll be there too if that will make you feel more comfortable."

"Actually, it would. Thank you."

"Not a problem." I heard a loud buzz in the background and Cade said, "I've got to go. My nuked dinner is ready. I'll see you tomorrow, Hannah."

"Bye, Cade…and thanks again." Feeling melancholy after his call, I took the dog and cat outside into the side yard and played catch with Boone. Jig ate grass, then persistently chased a giant grasshopper. I watched in horror as he caught the bug and ate the poor thing.

CADE ARRIVED AT PRECISELY TEN THE NEXT MORNING, AND GUS PULLED IN behind him. I guided them to the fenced-in yard, and Gus grunted a couple of times and took several measurements—with Cade's assistance. The old man sketched onto his clipboard, scratched his balding head a few times, then drew some more. When he finished, he turned around and stared at the back of the cottage. Several expressions flitted across his face, and when I thought I noted a few tears in his eyes, he quickly turned away and pretended to peruse his clipboard once again.

Cade and I strolled to the back deck as we gave Gus the time he needed to collect himself. We talked randomly about the weather and other trivial things.

Gus finally ambled over to us and said gruffly, "I'll throw some ideas together and get back to you tomorrow." He stalked out of the side gate, and after a few minutes, we heard his truck leave.

"Well, that was charming," I replied.

Cade sighed and pursed his lips in frustration. "Sorry about that. There's something about this place that shoves him into overdrive. I'll ask him again if he wants to do the landscaping."

"That may be a good idea. By the way, do you know anyone I can hire to manage the mowing and trimming of my yard? After this latest rain, my property looks more like a hay field than a lawn."

Cade grinned, then replied, "Huey's always looking for extra work and he mows for a retired couple a few miles down the road. I'll ask him and let you know."

"Thanks, Cade, I'd appreciate it." I figured he'd leave soon, so I devised an idea. "Would you like to go for a walk with Boone and me? The trails are beautiful and I'd love for you to join us." My face blushed and I glanced away. *How does this man make me feel like a silly schoolgirl?*

When I didn't hear a response, I looked back at Cade and discovered him staring at me, apparently taken aback by my request. "I think I have some extra time and would love to."

I smiled in happiness and went inside to retrieve Boone. Removing his offending cone from his head, we walked back outside, and Cade joined us on our stroll. We talked endlessly about everything under the sun, and Boone excitedly ran back and forth, sniffing everything in sight. Cade and I stopped to watch a couple of vibrant swallowtail butterflies, and we were only distracted for a moment. Unfortunately, when we turned, Boone had vanished. We called him several times, but he didn't return. I was frantic, but Cade said not to worry and that he'd help me find him.

"Boone! Come!" I yelled over and over again. After a few moments, I heard a rustling, and he finally appeared around a large thicket of dense bushes with something in his mouth. Trotting up to us, he carefully laid the item at our feet.

"Oh my gosh, Boone! What have you done?" It was a baby raccoon and its eyes weren't yet open. It laid at our feet, squirming slightly, and we noticed a few drops of smeared blood on the side of its head.

Cade bent down and touched the animal. It squeaked and tried to nurse on Cade's finger. "The blood doesn't seem to be coming from him. We need to return it to its mother, Hannah."

I stared at Boone and said, "My dear boy, you must take us to where you found him. Do you understand?"

"Arf!" He backed up hurriedly, barking frantically as if he wanted us to follow him. Cade picked up the raccoon and we followed Boone back into the deep woods.

After several minutes, I wondered if he was leading us on a wild goose chase, but then we saw something ahead. As we neared it, we realized the mother raccoon had passed away. Huddled against her were three more kits, but it looked like two of them were already dead—killed by the same predator that had taken the mother's life.

"What do we do, Cade?"

"I suggest we take the two that are still alive back to your place and call the local vet. She'll know what to do."

Boone stood near the kits, apparently wanting to ensure we would care for the little buggers. I picked up the other live one and we hurried back to the cottage. Calling Dr. Neumann, she instructed us to bring them right in and she'd examine the poor babies. We wrapped them in towels to keep them warm and let the kits snuggle together. Cade drove us in his truck, and when we arrived at the vet's office, we were guided to an exam room.

The kind vet examined them and said they appeared to be fine, other than dehydrated and needing sustenance.

"Why don't you leave them here until tomorrow, and my staff and I will get them hydrated and fed. Then you can take them home and care for them until I can find a rehabber who has an opening." I stared at Dr. Neumann as if she'd grown two heads.

"What? I don't know anything about caring for wild animals. Can you find someone else to take them in?" Even to my ears, I heard the panic in my voice.

Dr. Neumann placed a calming hand on my shoulder and said, "Hannah, it's not rocket science. You must bottle-feed them every few hours and keep them warm and contained. Of course, you'll have to clean them periodically—which is what their mother would do. I'll give you detailed instructions as well as bottles and formula. Yes, it's a commitment, but I don't have anyone else to care for them. I'd also say their eyes will open in approximately one more week, so at least you have that going for you."

Cade must have seen the terror in my eyes and said, "Hannah, I'll help. I've done this before and also know how to care for them. We'll work out the details by the time we pick them up tomorrow."

Gazing into his gorgeous brown eyes, I sighed in relief and thanked him repeatedly.

AS CADE DROVE ME HOME FROM THE VET'S OFFICE, HE SAID HE'D rearrange his schedule so he could help with the kits. Cade also informed me that he had his dog to tend to at his house, so he'd have to drive back and forth between our homes.

"What? You have a dog? Gee willikers, why didn't you tell me? You never mentioned it, and I'd love it if you could tell me about him—uh —her...."

Cade grinned wryly and replied, "It's a him. His name is Milo and he's a four-year-old Corgi. I guess the fact never came up in conversation. Anyway, my dad gave him to me two years ago when the puppy was abandoned at the town cemetery. He's the sweetest dog and loves everyone."

"I can't wait to meet him, Cade." I pondered the situation for a few minutes, then sat up straighter in my seat and turned to Cade, giving him a huge grin.

He looked at me with an arched eyebrow. "What?" he asked suspiciously.

"I have an idea. Now hear me out before you say no."

He nodded and waited.

"I have a huge home with plenty of room, and I need a lot of help with those baby raccoons."

"Uh-huh," he said as he waited for me to continue.

"How about...you take the downstairs bedroom and stay with me until the coons are big enough for us to release? You can also bring Milo. I know Boone would love him, and you know Jig doesn't care if there's another dog. What do you say?"

"Hannah..."

"Cade, there's nothing untoward in this invitation. It's simply that I need help and can't do this alone." The thought of caring for these wild animals made my heart race, and I was already chewing on my fingernails from anxiety.

The way he looked at me, Cade realized I was correct. Panic mode filled me with knowing I'd have to take on the additional responsibilities of caring for these wild babies.

Cade turned his attention back to the road. His eyebrows lowered and he pursed his lips in thoughtful contemplation. After a few minutes, he finally replied. "Okay. But I'll pay for my expenses and will also help around the house—you know, like cooking and cleaning. Luckily these babies grow pretty fast, and let me tell you, raccoons get into everything once they get big enough, so the sooner we release them, the better."

I exhaled loudly and said, "Thanks, Cade. You don't know what this means to me." Wiggling in my seat, I couldn't contain my relief and happiness. But then, I realized what I had done. I'd invited a man—who I barely knew—to live with me in my home. *Come on, Hannah, Cade's a good man. But I've been wrong so many times when judging men. What if I'm making another mistake?*

But that little crack in my wall that had held God at bay seemed to say, "Trust yourself, child. He'll save your life." I cocked my head in confusion, then decided to believe the voice in my head. Fear and anxiety that had once filled my psyche finally departed.

That afternoon, Cade moved himself and his dog into my place. Boone welcomed his new playmate with an excited tail and kept bumping poor Milo with his e-collar. However, Cade's dog patiently accepted his new friend and didn't seem to mind the continued *whop* of the plastic cone. Even Jig welcomed Milo with a sniff and a gentle head-butt, then took off to play with his catnip mouse.

Cade kept his word, helped with the cat and dogs, and even cooked dinner that evening. I cleaned up and took care of the dishes, and we spent the evening watching another John Wayne movie on the television. The dogs happily played with their toys on the floor and Jig was fast asleep on Cade's lap. I contentedly leaned against Cade's shoulder as everything appeared to be going so well. *Or was it?*

Chapter Fifteen

The next day, we picked up the kits from the vet, and Dr. Neumann showed us how to feed and care for the little rascals. She also provided detailed instructions and said to call her if we needed anything. But what went through my mind was, *please take care of them for me!* I bit my lip and kept my mouth shut.

Cade told Dr. Neumann that we already had an adequate cage and bedding for the kits and would be fine. I glared silently at Cade, and he stared back with innocently raised eyebrows. *The dirtbag! Albeit a gorgeous one.*

After we arrived back at the cottage, Cade helped me bring in one of the cages and set it up for the raccoons. They slept soundly as we laid them in their new enclosure on a large shelf in the laundry room.

Jig jumped onto the shelf, sniffed the critters in the cage, then turned around and stalked off in an apparent huff.

"I hope Jig's not going to be a problem. These poor babies have been through enough without a cat attacking them," I said, followed by a heavy sigh.

Cade agreed we should keep a close eye on them. But when we pulled them out of their cage a few hours later for their feeding, Jig surprised us. We sat on the sofa with one kit wrapped in a towel on each of our laps, and Jig jumped up and cautiously moved over to sniff them again, but this time, he licked them carefully and then snuggled up to the one in my lap.

"Well, what do ya know? Jig wants to help care for them," Cade replied in shock.

"Cade, is it okay to name the raccoons?"

"I don't see why not. We must remember they'll be released into the wild once they're old enough. Why? Do you have ideas for their names?"

"Yup. I was thinking Widget for the darker one and Whatcha for the other."

"I get Widget, but Whatcha?"

"Yes. It's short for What-cha-ma-call-it."

Cade snickered and said, "I like it! Good job, my love!" He leaned over and kissed me passionately, but the kits grew impatient for their food and tried to squirm away.

I smiled with glee from his kiss and we finished feeding the raccoons. Jig took over cleaning the kits, and the dogs were careful and kind to the baby raccoons.

That evening, I prepared dinner and we sat at the table enjoying our spaghetti. Cade told stories about his adventures growing up around animals and how he learned the construction trade from his father.

"Hannah, I was thinking. I've been taking horse therapy from a stable just outside of town, and it's helped me with my issues, and I wondered if you'd like to go with me?" I gave him a skeptical eyebrow. But he raised his hand, stopping my instant objection. "All I ask is that you give it a try. What do you have to lose?"

"Life and limb for one. And two—well, I think number one is enough." I stared at him as if he'd grown two heads.

His dark eyes flashed, daring me to continue my objections. "The horses are gentle, and the staff is well trained in helping veterans and anyone dealing with painful psychological issues. Come on, what do ya say?" His charming grin caused my toes to curl inside my tennis shoes.

"I...don't know. I've never touched a horse before nor ridden one either. Frankly, it sounds terrifying."

"You don't ride them right away—if at all. It's learning to communicate and work with them. Hannah, you won't have to do anything you don't want to. Nothing is forced on you."

"Okay. But I'm trusting you on this and that I don't have to ride a wild, homicidal stallion around a track the first day. If that happens, I'll make you pay for it, bub!" When I stressed my point, I shook my fork at him as a warning, and spaghetti flew across the table and landed on Cade's nose and shirt. The pasta hung from his face, and he crossed his eyes, trying to look at the noodles dangling off his nose.

I laughed so hard I thought I'd snort spaghetti from my nostrils. Cade guffawed at the look on my face. He then picked up a meatball and tossed it onto my shirt with a loud *splat*. My giggles stopped in shock but then picked up again when the two dogs began chomping on the food that landed on the floor.

"Oh my, Cade. What are we doing?" I snickered again and the grin on Cade's face was priceless and full of mischief. He reached over to pick up the cherry tomatoes from the salad and aimed at my head. I squealed with delight and jumped from my chair to flee the offending red missiles. He chased me into the living room and I dodged behind the sofa. He came around the side, and I realized he was out of ammo.

"You dirty dog! Why—I'll have you know I'm deadly with iceberg lettuce—you varmint!" I ran back to the kitchen counter, grabbed what was left of the head of lettuce and took aim. Cade followed me, looking for something else to throw. Tossing up his hands in defeat, he grinned mischievously and took off into the living room again, laughing maniacally like a dastardly villain.

I ran after him. When he turned to face me, I threw the lettuce hard, hitting him squarely in the chest. After seeing the wet spot on his shirt and the spaghetti sauce, he slowly and deliberately approached me and roughly pulled me into his arms for a long and passionate kiss. I couldn't contain myself and buried my hands in his thick, silky hair, keeping his mouth on mine and devouring it even more.

We panted with passion when we finally pulled apart. He gazed intently into my eyes, but his serious expression returned to mirth.

"What?" I asked, placing my hands on my hips in a threatening stance.

"Your face is covered in tomato sauce and one piece of pasta." His chuckle was infectious, and I stomped to the bathroom to take a look. He followed me and I saw him in the mirror behind me. Cade was correct. Food covered us both.

I giggled again, then bent over the sink to wash off the red smear of sauce. When I turned around, I handed Cade a wet washcloth for him to wipe his face. But once I faced him, he put a hand on each side of the sink, trapping me with my back against it.

"Hannah, you're one amazing and stunning woman. Where have you been all my life?" His comment and stare left me breathless and I didn't know how to respond. So, I kept silent.

Cade moved in again for another earth-shaking kiss. This one was slow and all-consuming. I felt my knees buckle, but Cade broke the contact, backed up with a tender smile, and left the room.

I stood still momentarily, then quietly moved to shut the door and looked into the mirror. My face was red with passion and my lips were swollen from Cade's heated kisses. Turning on the faucet again, I splashed cold water on my flushed skin, then tried to remove the food stains from my t-shirt.

What am I going to do? I'm crazy about this man and I may still be married to a lunatic. Cade knows nothing about me and I don't know if I dare tell him who I really am. You're in a real pickle, Hannah.

That night, Cade offered to take care of the kits' feedings. I gladly consented and went upstairs to bed. Boone joined me, but Jig insisted on staying with Cade and the raccoons.

When I came downstairs the following day, I found Cade asleep on the sofa. I caught my breath when I spotted him. He only wore a pair of pajama bottoms and was stretched out blissfully in sleep, with one arm thrown casually over his head. Simply staring at his muscled tanned chest, I imagined what it would feel like to snuggle against him and what may come after. Old scars marked his skin along the front of his right shoulder, which appeared to be from a couple of bullet wounds. I desperately wanted to kiss those marks away and began to lean forward. But shaking my head, I reprimanded myself and shifted my gaze to the end of the sofa.

The kits snuggled happily inside a stack of towels, and Jig curled himself around them in a nest of protection. Upon my approach, my kitty raised his head and peered at me with his sleepy, bright green eyes. He chirped a greeting and returned to nestle closer to the babies.

I moved nearer to Cade and gazed at his face. Very gently, I moved a stray strand of soft, dark hair away from his forehead. The dark morning stubble enhanced his rugged good looks, and I wished I could lean down and stroke his firm, masculine jaw.

Sighing regretfully, I entered the kitchen to prepare the raccoons' breakfast. I scrambled several eggs, tossed in some leftover ham and cheese, and whipped up an omelet. A strong pair of arms came around me from behind as I finished at the stove, and a rough cheek rubbed against mine.

"I hope that's you, Cade, and not a porcupine." I heard a chuckle behind me, and he placed a sweet kiss on my neck.

"Are you calling me prickly?"

I refused to turn around because I feared he'd continue to kiss me, and things would go too far. "I call 'em like I see 'em."

"Touché. Breakfast smells great, but give me a few minutes for a quick shower and shave."

Finally turning around, I commented, "Who said these eggs are for you?" I snorted, and he gave me a playful wink and left the room.

I sighed heavily again at his departing mouthwatering body and drop-dead good looks.

"Arf, arf!" Two dogs stood at my feet, begging for their breakfast. The spell vanished and I had to feed the brood. Even Jig showed up waiting for kibble. He belted out a loud howl.

"Alright, already! It's coming!" Laughing at their exuberance, I fed them and the kits. Once the raccoons were safely back in their cage, it was time to feed Cade and me.

The remainder of the day settled into a routine, and we took turns caring for the babies. Cade was a considerate houseguest and helped with my usual chores. He even offered to pick up the dogs' droppings in the yard. I found his offer a great relief to my sensibilities, although I heard a few gagging noises as he picked up the offending piles.

In the afternoon, Gus showed up with his landscape ideas. Sitting at the kitchen table with us, he reviewed his plan, and his politeness surprised me. I eagerly agreed to his proposal and the cost, and he said he could start in a couple of days.

Cade and I enjoyed another dinner together, and this time, he cooked. The aroma of the perfectly seasoned pot roast filled the room. His talent in the kitchen impressed me and I told him so.

"I have many skills, Hannah—some I'd love to demonstrate for you." He wiggled his eyebrows and I couldn't stop my laughter.

"I'm sure you would." I rolled my eyes in exasperation, then said, "I have to say, I'm thrilled you can cook, plus you volunteer to pick up dog poo. That alone makes you a winner in my book, Cade." Giving him a "thumbs-up," I ignored his suggestive comment and continued the fine meal.

"Alright, I'll behave, Hannah. But darn, you take all the fun out of being frisky!" He gave me a goofy smile and I giggled at his antics.

That night, Cade helped me take the kits upstairs because it was my turn to feed them at regular intervals. He said goodnight and wished me luck.

The feedings and bathing went well with the kits, and after the second time, I fell into a deep sleep.

THE DREAM STARTS AGAIN WITH TRACE AND ME AT THE BLUFFS. BUT HIS *face turns into a demon when he's on top of me during our ground tussle. His eyes are blazing red, and huge fangs protrude from his mouth, dripping with saliva. I can smell a horrific stench as he grinds his body into mine.*

His breath is rank as he spits the words into my face, "You're mine, and you'll never get away from me. Not even in death, you filthy piece of camel dung. You'll never get away from me. I own you for all eternity." He dips his head to pierce my cheek with his massive, pointed teeth and rips a chunk off my face. I scream in terror and agony.

"HANNAH—WAKE UP! YOU'RE HAVING A NIGHTMARE, SWEETIE." I SAT UP jerkily in bed. Cade was sitting next to me and had been shaking me awake. My body shuddered because of the horrible nightmare, and by the look on Cade's face, he was terrified by the panic in my eyes.

"Cade…it's so awful. I thought I'd killed him…it was an accident…at least, the news says he's dead…but I'm still not sure. What if he isn't? It's never going to be over!"

"Shh. It's okay, sweetheart. I promise it'll be okay. Now there…." He pulled me close into his arms and rubbed my back in comfort.

"You don't understand—it'll never be okay. No matter what I do, I can't escape the abuse. My stepfather…then Trace. Why do men hurt me? What did I do to deserve this? Why did God let all this happen to me?"

"Oh baby, I'm so sorry." He backed up a couple of inches to wipe the tears from my face. "I don't know why these men hurt you, but I can tell you this, God doesn't *let* anything happen. Men did this, not God." He kissed the tears away, laid beside me on the bed, and pulled me close. "One thing you can count on, sweetheart, is I will never let anyone hurt you again. You can take that to the bank, honey."

"You can't promise that, Cade. No one can. If my husband is still alive, he *will* find me and kill me. He owns the town and everyone in it—including the law. If he's actually dead, his evil family may want me dead too—if they don't believe that was my body burned to a crisp at the quarry. Then it would only be a matter of time before they find me."

Cade's body had stiffened and he stopped rubbing my back.

"Cade?"

"You're married, Hannah?" I sat up quickly and drew my knees to my chest.

"Yes. Such as it is…or was. I tried to tell you not to get involved with me and that it could never work. I am—or was—married to a criminal who has or had an evil criminal family and enterprise. His family also owns the town where we lived and everyone in it. It's such a mess!"

Cade sat up too, not saying a word. I watched his face under the light of the bedside lamp, trying to gauge his reaction to my confession. Waiting for his response was more terrifying than tonight's nightmare. His expression changed from shock to anger, then to resignation. He rose from the bed and I knew it was over.

"I'm so sorry, Cade. I never meant to hurt you. You're an amazing man who shouldn't be involved in my problems. Don't worry, I'll take care of the kits, and you can return to your home tomorrow—I completely understand." I was now talking to Cade's bare back as he had turned on the bed with his feet on the floor, facing away from me.

"Hannah…." I watched as he ran a frustrated hand through his tousled hair and stood up to leave. But he turned to look at me. His expression was guarded, and I had no clue what he was thinking.

"It's okay, Cade."

"No…Hannah, I need time to digest this. I won't rush into any decisions or judgments until you tell me everything, and tonight is not the right time. Let's both get some rest and we can talk tomorrow. *Capiche?*"

I didn't say anything for a few moments because I was surprised by his comments. Then, a small glimmer of hope ran through me, and I finally replied, *"Capiche."*

After he left my room, I couldn't fall back to sleep. Tears slipped down my cheeks as I contemplated what may happen tomorrow morning, and I dreaded his possible reaction to everything I had to tell him. *Would he dump me, or would he stay?*

Chapter Sixteen

The next morning, I anxiously waited to see Cade. I wondered if I'd lost a good friend. But it wasn't an issue, as he came upstairs to assist me in bringing the kits to the first floor. He greeted me with a smile, although it wasn't as warm as I'd hoped.

After we fed the animals and ourselves, Cade asked me to join him on the sofa. He patted the seat beside him, but I said it would be better if I took the chair.

He looked hurt, so I quickly replied, "Cade, I can think more clearly if there's some space between us—and I know you understand what I mean." I lowered my eyes with embarrassment, and he kindly told me it was fine.

I swallowed hard and wrung my hands several times before explaining. "Maybe I should start at the beginning, and it may take some time to get through everything." Glancing at him under my eyelashes, he nodded, giving me time to gather my thoughts. I rubbed my sweaty palms on the legs of my jeans and cleared my throat.

"My early childhood was wonderful—at least what I can remember. My birth dad doted on me and I loved him dearly. Back then, my mother was attentive and loving."

I proceeded to tell him about my dad's sudden death and how my mother withdrew from life and me.

"When my mom met my soon-to-be stepfather, she came alive again. But it was only for him. He was a deacon of his church and well-respected by his peers. When he and my mom grew closer, she became a religious zealot, consistently quoted the Bible, and adorned our entire household with religious icons. She never returned to the loving and caring mother I once knew and loved. My stepfather and Jesus were all that mattered to her.

"It wasn't long before my stepfather took a sexual interest in me. When my mom started working the night shift, he took advantage of us being alone." I stopped for a few minutes, unsure how to continue telling my life story. "It started with innuendo, then turned to porn videos, and he'd ask me if I'd like that done to me. Needless to say, I found it disgusting and told him so."

I stood and began pacing the room. Avoiding Cade's gaze, I moved back and forth, summoning the courage to continue.

"It's okay, Hannah. You don't have to go on if it's too difficult." Cade's voice was quiet and sympathetic, yet calming.

"I feel I have to, Cade." Stealing a glance at him, I read his compassion and patience and continued. "When he started molesting me, I told my mother. But confiding in her was a major mistake. She shrieked and called me every name in the book, saying that Satan had taken possession of me and to leave her husband alone. She also claimed I tempted him, that he was weak and couldn't resist the devil's...lure...." My voice hitched as I hiccupped a sob of despair.

Instantly, Cade stood beside me and pulled me gently into his arms. "Hannah, I'm so sorry. You were just a baby, and they both should have been throttled and thrown into prison."

I snuggled into his warm embrace. Speaking into his shoulder, I continued, "I guess I was lucky because he never actually raped me. Something always seemed to interrupt his final goal of assaulting me. My mom would come home unexpectedly, or someone would knock at the door. But I knew it was only a matter of time, so I finally ran away."

Stepping out of his arms, I sat down, but this time, Cade joined me.

"I lived on the streets until a cop found me, and I entered the system. I did well there and was sent to some decent foster homes. When I aged out, I found an adequate job and worked hard to get my B.A. degree in English Literature. After graduating, I moved to Nevada for a great paying job. That's when I met Trace. We hit it off right away and I thought I was in love. What more could a girl want than a good-looking, wealthy, well-respected man? It was a whirlwind relationship and before I knew it, we were married.

"Trace treated me well for the first couple of months of our marriage, but I already knew something was off. He insisted I quit my job and no longer connect with friends from work, and I found him looking through my phone. I also noticed he conducted strange meetings in the middle of the night. Odd and nefarious people came to the house, and I wasn't allowed to ask about them or what they may have discussed. Obviously, it was all illegal and dangerous.

"One night, when I began pushing Trace to tell me what was going on, he hit me and screamed at the top of his lungs. After the first few times he punched me, I tried to stay quiet and always did what he said. But that didn't matter. If he was in a bad mood, I became his punching bag. Finally, I went to the sheriff, and to my dismay, I discovered Trace and his family owned the police, the local D.A., and the judge."

I halted telling my story and peered at Cade. Sadness, anger, and frustration filled his handsome face. He took my hands and said, "I don't know what to say, Hannah. What you've endured is made of nightmares, and I understand why you're cautious about trusting anyone. But you need to know that I'm here for you and will do anything to protect you from harm. I hope you believe me, sweetheart." His last words seemed to be forced from his mouth, and when I gazed into his eyes, I knew why. Tears pooled there. It took me by surprise and I also cried. He snuggled me close and we sobbed together.

When we pulled apart, he caressed my face. I then told him how I met a nurse at a hospital who introduced me to Kogi and, ultimately, my plan to run away from my abusive and controlling husband. Holding nothing back, I told him about the night I left Trace, the altercation at the bluffs, how he'd fallen over the cliff, and the recent news items. When I finished, Cade kissed my cheek and stood up. He walked to the large back window, staring at the glistening lake.

I rose from the couch and joined him. Taking his hand, I guided him outside, and the dogs followed. We went down to the beach and sat together on the soft sand, not saying a word and letting the beauty of the scene before us heal our grief.

After the dogs romped in the water, they sat beside us and fell asleep on the warm sand.

"Hannah, how did you end up here at Storm Harbor?"

I explained the strange and timely gift of the cottage by an unknown benefactor.

"That *is* bizarre," he said. "But I must say, what a blessing for both of us. I wouldn't have ever met you." He kissed my hand again, then held it to his heart.

"Cade?"

"Hmm?"

"We have to feed the kits."

He made a rude noise, then smiled at me after glancing at his silver watch. "So, we do."

We stood and strolled to the cottage with the dogs following closely behind. Cade stopped momentarily, turned to me, and said confidently, "Hannah, we'll figure this out. I have connections in high places and we'll take your husband's crew out permanently. There's *always* a solution."

"Thanks, Cade. But this isn't your problem. It's—"

"Don't say it! Your problems are my problems, so don't even say it!" Cade's response had a harsh edge, but he took a few deep breaths and started again, using a much calmer timbre, "Hannah, I know we haven't known each other long, but it doesn't matter. You've become a significant part of my life, and I have no intention of letting anything happen to you. He's already stolen too much from you, and his cohorts aren't taking anything else. Let me work on it, and we'll devise a viable plan, and you'll be kept in the loop."

I hugged him close and hot tears pooled in my eyes once more.

The crack grew wider around my soul. *Did God really do this? Did He protect me all the years from an even worse fate? Could Cade help me?*

Who were these connections he talked about? Could they be trusted? I knew I had to rely on someone because I could no longer live like this— letting fear and mistrust rule every decision and move I made.

God, if you're truly there, I'm laying all this at your feet because I can no longer do this alone.

Chapter Seventeen

The next day, Cade decided to run errands and would be gone for several hours. I said it wouldn't be a problem and I could handle all the feedings for the day. The kits' eyes were finally open and we'd start them on the solid foods the vet recommended. Unfortunately, the little raccoons' behaviors changed from slow to rambunctious, and they wanted to explore their new world—much to our dismay. The little critters' energy made them difficult to contain, and we sighed in relief when they finally fell asleep in exhaustion.

Gus arrived with Huey in tow, and they had a truckload of landscape supplies, soil, and many colorful plants and flowers. Gus said he'd have everything done within the next two days.

"I can't wait to see the finished garden, Gus. And your choice of purple irises is the bomb. It looks like you brought plants that will bloom throughout all three seasons!" I said excitedly with a side of teasing.

"Of course I did—I always have dinkum good ideas," he replied gruffly. He tried to hide it, but I caught his grin of pride when he turned away.

After feeding the kits in the afternoon, I returned them to their cage and decided to take Boone and Milo for a walk. The dogs chased each other around my feet and I had to get them outside for some exercise.

I went upstairs to change and checked my hidden cell phone in case there were any messages. One new text from Kogi flashed brightly, and my stomach tightened in apprehension.

"Just thought you should know that Cameron's been out of town for the last couple of days, and no one knows where he went or why. My instincts tell me it wasn't for anything good. Stay vigilant, my dear girl. I'll contact you if I learn anything more."

Texting him with a quick "thank you," I put the phone on the charger, changed my clothes, and headed back downstairs.

"Come on, you two. Let's get some air."

"Arf!" Boone danced around my feet again, and Milo twirled in circles in anticipation of the outing.

"We'll be back soon, Jig. Hold the fort!" The fluffy ball of fur sat contentedly on the dryer in one of his cat beds and blinked at me with his usual arrogant attitude. I knew what he was thinking...*Don't let the door hit your tush on the way out.* After kissing the top of his furry head, the dogs and I wandered out and followed our usual path into the woods.

It wasn't long before Lois made her presence known. "Hi, Hannah! I see you have an extra fur-butt with you today."

"Yeah. My horde appears to be growing—much to my dismay. This is Cade's dog, Milo." The two pups excitedly greeted Lois and she scratched and hugged both canines with kindness.

"I hope you'll join us, Lois."

"Thanks. I do believe I will. We can head over to our secluded place on the beach."

"That sounds like a plan," I replied, grinning happily.

As we strolled through the woods, we enjoyed the scent of pine, dried leaves, and wildflowers. Boone and Milo moved from one bush and tree to another, sniffing intently for whatever dogs discovered through their fabulous noses.

Strolling through the clearing, Lois and I took a seat on the driftwood and appreciated the beauty of our surroundings. I pulled out two worn tennis balls from my pockets and we tossed them for the pups to retrieve. They yapped in delight.

Lois chuckled at their antics and said, "The Lord has given us a delightful day, hasn't He?"

"That He has," I replied, then wondered why I agreed so quickly and my face flushed.

Lois turned to me and smiled with understanding. She hooked her arm through mine and we sat quietly for several minutes.

"Hannah, I'm thrilled to see you so happy. I've prayed constantly that you'd find Him. Don't be embarrassed by your feelings and never apologize for them, my dear."

"Lois, I'm not sure what I believe. I have to say, though, my heart feels lighter now that I told Cade about my past. But the doubts still linger about whether I made a mistake in confiding in him. Trust is not something I give lightly." Staring out toward the lake, I watched the waves sparkling in the bright sunlight, although the water had turned turbulent and dark.

"That's understandable, honey. But you have excellent instincts and the person you need to learn to trust is you. It'll come."

The dogs settled down onto the sand at our feet and panted with exhaustion. After a few moments, they fell asleep in apparent contentment. As I stared at them, it was as if they had grins plastered on their adorable mugs as they snoozed.

I commented, "Lois, the water is wilder today."

"Yes. There's another storm brewing and it'll be arriving soon."

"How do you know that? There wasn't anything on the local news."

"When you live on this lake long enough, you begin to read and understand it. Of course, my juju brain also helps me to gauge the forecast."

I laughed and squeezed her arm. "Yeah, you cheat!"

She giggled in response and said, "Archie always said that too—that I cheat." Her comment formed a huge, melancholy grin on her beautiful, regal face.

"Who's Archie?"

"The love of my life, dear. I guess you could say he's the one who got away."

"I'm so sorry, Lois."

"It's okay. That was years ago and I've moved on, but you never forget your true love. Archie was unlike any man I'd ever known. Of course, I thought he had everything—good looks, intelligence, talent, and charm, but he could be as stubborn as a mule, which caused a constant rift between us. He'd been married before and his wife cheated on him within the first year of their marriage. After divorcing her, he vowed to remain a bachelor and stay away from women.

"We met when we were in our fifties and he refused to ask me out for over a year. But finally, he did. It was kismet after that first date and we became inseparable. But his perpetual fear and doubt hung over our relationship, so he refused to ask me to marry him. I didn't care and wanted to be with him. For years, that's what we did. We were best friends and loved each other dearly—although he refused to verbally declare his love for me. But I knew.

"One day, when Archie was out of town on business, an old beau of mine, David, showed up out of the blue and we met for lunch. His sister and I had been best friends since childhood, and she had recently died from uterine cancer. She wrote me a letter from her deathbed telling me she'd left me some of her personal items. I only met with David so he could give them to me. Right after our meeting, he left town." Lois stared at the water, and her lovely face grimaced in emotional pain.

"As soon as Archie returned, the town gossip already told him about me meeting with a man, and he flew off the handle. He yelled and cursed at me and said I was like all the other women. I couldn't get a single word in, and I knew it was over. My heart broke and I knew I'd never change his mind."

I squeezed Lois's hand in comfort and when she turned to look at me, her beautiful brown eyes swam with tears. She quickly blinked them away and gave me a bright smile.

"I never married or had children in my lifetime, but that's what was meant to be. Don't get me wrong, Hannah, I've had a wonderful life with many amazing friends. And I also appreciate every moment God gave me with Archie. I just pray he'll let his anger and frustration go and enjoy the life he has left. It would be such a waste if he can't."

"I understand. Does he live around here?"

At that moment, a loud boom echoed across the lake and I jumped in surprise. The dogs did as well.

"We'd better go, my dear. This storm waits for no man—or woman. Let's move out."

Lois and I hugged and parted ways halfway back to the cottage.

"Take care of yourself, Lois, and I'll see you soon."

"You too, my dear." She gave me an odd look for a moment, then said, "When you get home, be sure to lock your doors and windows. You'll be okay, Hannah. Trust me." With a wave, she hurried off and disappeared into the woods. I shook my head in confusion at her instruction but figured she was being motherly.

The thunder clapped louder, and I told the dogs, "Let's get moving, babies, before the rain starts."

We made it home just in time. Luckily, Gus and Huey were gone for the day because of the bad weather. I locked the back door and knew the front was still secured from when we left for our walk. The deluge pounded on the windows and some rain had gotten through before I could close them. I grabbed some towels and wiped up the water.

I heard a scraping sound coming from the front entry and saw a dark, unfamiliar shadow through the small security window of the steel door. Boone and Milo growled deeply in their throats, and the fur on their backs stood up in warning. The person at the door wasn't Cade, as the dogs never made these aggressive sounds when he arrived home. I ran up the stairs to my room with the pups close on my heels and headed to the closet. Quickly opening a box on the top shelf, I pulled out a small handgun. Checking to make sure it was loaded, I flicked off the safety.

The storm's fury resounded overhead as it released its violent rampage of temper. The thundering booms and torrents of rain rattled the windows. But the crack of the front door being knocked down could still be heard. I hustled the dogs up the stairs to the third-floor attic and secured the steel hatch door into place. Gathering us together, we huddled down behind several stacked folding tables along the wall. My rapid breathing and racing heart echoed in my ears.

Flash...creak...boom! After hearing the loud creak between the rounds of thunder, it was apparent the intruder was coming up the first flight of stairs. *Meow...hiss...yowl!* A loud commotion echoed up the stairwell, and several vulgar swear words resounded from a deep male voice.

"Jig," I said silently, praying he was okay and the intruder didn't harm my sweet kitty. Grinding my teeth together—I now wanted to kill the creep.

"Serena…" The voice sang with condescension. "You're being rude by not greeting your guest. Come out, come out, wherever you are…." I didn't recognize the voice. The sound of doors opening and closing echoed up the stairwell as he searched the second floor.

Boone growled louder. "Shush, baby," I whispered. He whimpered in response and I hugged both dogs close to my side.

Pulling my phone from my pocket, I texted Cade. "Help! Intruder!"

"Coming," was his response. The phone vibrated again, saying, "Hide on the third floor and secure the hatch."

I typed, "Already there. I'm armed."

"Good. Hang on, babe."

Creak. The man moved up the stairs leading to the attic. Bile rose from my stomach and threatened to come into my throat. I swallowed it, firmly placed the pistol in both hands and aimed toward the hatch from behind the tables.

The storm still raged outside, but for some reason, I could no longer hear it. My attention honed in on the monster ascending the stairs.

"Serena…" he sang again. "You're a dead woman walking, so you might as well let me take you out quickly. Make it easier on yourself. The one who hired me said it was up to me to kill you fast or take my time. Now that I think about it, I could have fun with your luscious body."

Now at the top of the stairs, the monster attempted to open the hatch. I held the gun steady and couldn't believe they weren't shaking in terror. But Kogi trained me well in using all types of weapons. Taking a deep breath, I slowly released it and took a few more calming inhales of precious air.

Phump, phump! He fired at the hinges holding the hatch shut and it gave way. I knew that sound—it was a suppressor he'd attached to his weapon. The floorboards splintered from his bullets and he pushed the door open.

The dogs barked viciously in warning, but I urged them to stay behind me. Hearing more thumping from the lower floors, I had to ignore them and deal with the most imminent threat—the monster who was about to enter this room.

How dare he! Anger flooded me, and the adrenaline of fury moved through my body. I saw the hand and gun first, and it fired around the room in an attempt to take me down.

Yelling loudly as though I'd been shot, I waited to gauge his next move. "Please...don't hurt me," I whimpered, hoping it would tempt him to show himself. "I'll do anything you ask."

After a couple of moments, a head and upper chest popped up behind the hand and gun.

Boom, boom! I fired a couple of shots, and he disappeared as he tumbled down the stairs, and there was another thud as he hit bottom.

"Hannah!" Cade yelled from the floor below.

"I'm here!"

"Stay there until I tell you diff—" His words were cut off, then I heard several more gunshots.

When it finally grew quiet, I hollered, "Cade?"

No response.

"Cade, answer me!"

Chapter Eighteen

"Hannah, I'm here and okay, but the intruder isn't. He's dead. Put your weapon down, honey."

I heard footsteps again, but they stopped before reaching the top.

My shaking hand lowered the gun and I laid it at my feet. "Okay. It's on the floor." My hollow voice didn't sound like my own.

"That's good. I'm coming up now."

Cade's head appeared through the hatch and he spotted me peeking from behind the folded tables. Boone and Milo ran over to him, yelping for joy. Cade reached down and stroked the dogs in reassurance.

I stood up on shaky legs, but I was unable to move around the tables. Cade rushed over to me and pulled me into his arms.

"I'm okay, Cade. Really. I just…." My voice trailed off and I let myself melt into him and hung on to his muscular body. I hoped to absorb his strength.

After several minutes, he set me away and stared into my eyes. "Are you sure you aren't hurt?"

I nodded and realized my face was wet with tears. Angrily pushing the dampness away, I said, "I'm positive—but I'm furious!" Sheer rage had replaced my fear, and I began pacing the wooden floor. "Why can't they just leave me alone? They hired this maniac to kill me. I could spit, I'm so mad!"

"Hannah, it's okay." He tried to pull me back into his arms, but I evaded him. Cade persisted and held my struggling body close to his once more. I finally relented until I calmed down.

"Oh, Cade—you said he was dead? I killed him?"

"No—I did. You hit him twice in the shoulder, but he aimed for me when I reached the second-floor stairs. It's self-defense for both of us, sweetheart. Let's go downstairs and I'll need to call my brother. We'd better carry the dogs because I don't want them tracking through the crime scene."

I nodded numbly and we picked up the pups. Cade led me down the first set of stairs. The killer's body was sprawled on his back, and his eyes stared blindly at the ceiling. Blood pooled across his shirt, and the red mire covered the floor around him. I could still smell the acrid odor of gunfire and the new, unfamiliar pungent, and acidic stench of body fluids and death. A shudder went through me in response.

"Look only at me, Hannah," Cade whispered. But I couldn't tear my eyes away from the dead man. Luckily, I didn't recognize him, but his bloody face surprised me. There were long, grizzly claw marks from his forehead to his neck. Apparently, Jig was an excellent attack feline.

Cade guided me down the second set of stairs and toward the sofa in the living room.

"I have to find Jig!" Calling his name with a shaky voice, I finally spotted him as he crawled out from under the bookcase. His tail was immense and his eyes were as big as saucers. "Oh baby, come to momma, sweetie." He slinked over to me and I picked him up and hugged him to my chest. After crooning to him for a few minutes while checking him over for any injuries, he began to purr. Jig was uninjured, and I praised him for his heroics.

"Meoooww!"

"I know, baby—you did good!" He wanted down, paraded himself around my ankles, and howled again in triumph. I couldn't help but smile at his antics.

I sat on the sofa and the two dogs climbed onto my lap. Their little bodies still trembled from the violence that occurred in our home.

Cade dialed his phone as he strolled into the kitchen. He turned his back to me so I couldn't hear the conversation. After several minutes, he disconnected the call and returned to join me on the sofa.

After pulling me close again, he said, "Phoenix is on his way and will be here in about an hour. He'll help us deal with all of this."

"How? I mean, shouldn't we call 911?"

"I wouldn't advise it—at least, not until we speak with Phoenix. Hannah, you need to know that I already told my brother today about your situation, as well as the name of your abusive husband, his family, and the town they run."

When he saw the look of outrage on my face, he continued, "Before you get mad, let me finish. Phoenix is the Deputy Director at the FBI. Trust me when I say you're lucky to have him in your corner. If anyone can help you out of this mess, he can."

"Seriously?" I calmed down with the information he'd provided and I was hopeful.

"Yup. But we both shot a man and he's now dead. There's no getting around that fact. Do you have a license for your handgun?"

"Well…yes. But it's under my alias, so that could definitely be a problem." I stared off into space for a moment. *Would I be going to jail?*

"We'll figure it out. I'm licensed to carry being ex-military, but I still had to kill a man—or should I say, the intruder."

While we waited for Phoenix to arrive, Cade suggested I pack a bag because it would be wise for me to leave the house for a few days—at least, until we found out more about the assassin who tried to kill me. Cade waited outside my bedroom door while I packed, as he was still in protective mode. The dead body on this floor still gave me the willies, so I thanked him for staying close.

It wasn't long until the doorbell rang, and Phoenix stood there in a dark suit, looking stern and wearing a no-nonsense expression. I still wondered if Cade made an error in calling him.

"Cade, Hannah." Phoenix nodded to us with a scowl, and I stepped back in frustration.

"Phoenix," Cade answered. I nodded and waited for what was to come.

"You better take me to the body, brother," Phoenix said.

"Yep. This way. He's on the second-floor landing." I watched as they donned elastic shoe coverings and trudged up the stairs, but I decided I needed to monitor the situation.

Phoenix looked back at me and scowled again. "You better stay downstairs, Hannah."

"I don't think so, Phoenix. This is my can of worms and I intend to see it through."

His handsome face looked thoughtful for a moment, then he nodded, handed me a pair of shoe protectors, and we started up the stairs once more.

Once we reached the top of the landing, I stayed out of their way and watched intently. Phoenix put on a pair of latex gloves, took photos of the intruder, and searched the dead man's pockets. Phoenix found a small sheet of paper with my address and an attached image. He also discovered a phone in the killer's other pocket, and Phoenix took hold of the corpse's thumb and pressed it to the cell so it would unlock. Flipping through several screens and giving away no revealing expression, he slipped the evidence into protective bags, including the man's weapon.

"What happened to his face?" Phoenix asked as he stared speculatively at the man on the floor.

"It was the cat," Cade replied.

Phoenix chuckled and pulled a small gadget from his pocket. He took fingerprints from both of the dead man's hands. After slipping the device back into his jacket, he motioned us to return to the first floor.

We sat on the sofa, and Phoenix said, "I hate to tell you this, but I know this perp. He's well known in his field as a high-priced hitman and goes by the name Martin McKay. They call him "The Solver," and we've been after him for years. I can tell you right now we may not find anything on his phone, but we at least have to try. Amazingly, you two took him down—he must have been having an off day—luckily for you."

"A hitman?" I asked, and it only came out as a high squeak.

Phoenix nodded and said, "If your husband is dead, we must figure out who hired this mercenary. But whoever this guy worked for, I doubt he or whoever hired him would employ a second killer. At least, not yet. But this person will when the 'The Solver' doesn't contact them that the hit's been completed.

"Hannah, I suggest you leave for a few days and let me handle everything. But, I'll have to inform my team of your situation, and I mean all of the dirty laundry—your husband, his family, the town, your previous life, the cliff incident, your escape, and this hitman's demise. We'll handle it from here. Right now, I'll need to take an official statement from both of you."

Cade and I gave an account of what happened during the attack. Phoenix remained patient, asked several questions, and finally said we were done for now. He advised us to leave the cottage, so his people could do their jobs once they arrived.

"Where will you two be staying?" Phoenix asked.

"She'll be at my place for now. I'll pack my things and head out before your team arrives."

"But, Cade, what about the animals—the kits, cat, and dogs?" I asked fearfully.

"My folks will take care of the kits. The cat and dogs can come to my place. I'll call Huey to come to my house to pick up the kits and deliver them to my parents. I need you to pack up what you need for Boone and Jig."

I nodded as if on autopilot and followed his instructions.

Cade watched my numb expression, then stopped momentarily and cupped my face in his hands. He stared into my eyes and said, "It's okay, kiddo. You're safe and we've got you. Okay?"

After searching his face, I sighed deeply and realized I could trust this man with my life. After giving him a shaky smile, I nodded, and he kissed me. Moving away, I did as he instructed and gathered what the animals would need at their new locations.

It didn't take long to pack up and load up both vehicles. Cade had me follow him to his home. But after several minutes on the road, I quickly pulled over, jumped out of the car, and vomited several times. Cade rushed to my side and rubbed my back in compassion.

"Are you alright?" he asked quietly.

I only nodded in response. When I finished purging my last meal, I sat down on my rump in the gravel on the side of the road. Cade quietly sat beside me and pulled me close. My hands and the rest of my body shook in earnest again. I was breathing too fast and it made me lightheaded.

"It'll get better, sweetheart. I promise. You've been through so much and you'll get through this. Hannah, you're my beautiful warrior." Cade kissed my temple and we sat there for several minutes, holding one another. My shaking hands and panicked breathing finally settled.

"We need to get moving. Are you okay now?" he whispered gently into my ear.

"Yes. Cade—if I've never said it before—thanks."

His eyes sparkled in kindness, and he replied, "You're welcome."

We climbed back into our vehicles and arrived at Cade's home within twenty minutes. The drive gave me time to think about how this assassin found me. *Was it Cameron who hired the hitman? Could this have been what Kogi worried about when Cameron was out of town?* But I still had no clue by the time we arrived at Cade's home.

His place was a sprawling ranch-style home hidden within a large wooded area. I found it delightful. We brought the animals into the house, as well as my luggage.

"Wow, your home is stunning!" I couldn't contain my joy at the masculine sprawling furniture, hardwood floors, cathedral ceiling of the great room, and the massive windows surrounding the place. The view of the woods gave us a sense of peace, and I even spotted a few deer off the back deck.

"Thanks." He winked, then continued, "Come, I'll take you to your room. There's an attached bath, so you should have everything you need."

I followed him down a hallway to the right of the great room. "This is my room," he said as we passed a sizeable primary suite on the left. "Your room is at the end of the hall."

This bedroom had been decorated in lovely restful hues of green. The bed faced a French door, which led to a small balcony.

"Cade, thank you. It's beautiful."

"I like it too."

Jig and Boone must have finished exploring the house and checked out this bedroom. Boone carried his pot-bellied pig and gave it a loud squeak each time he found something fascinating. Milo followed the other two animals around as he must have thought they were playing a game.

"I'd say Jig and Boone love your place as well," I said with a giggle. Cade smiled and petted Jig after he jumped onto the bed and plopped down in satisfaction.

"You don't say? When you're finished, join me in the great room while we wait for Huey's arrival."

"Will do."

After unpacking, I used the bathroom, and when I viewed my reflection in the mirror, I gasped—there wasn't a bit of color in my cheeks. Pulling out my makeup case, I added several layers of blush so I wouldn't look like a cast member from the *Walking Dead* series.

I found Cade sitting on the sofa feeding the kits.

"Do you need any help?" I asked as I joined him on the couch.

"Nope. I'm good. Widget's the last one to be fed."

A knock sounded at the door and I looked fearfully at Cade.

"Who is it?" he yelled.

"It's Huey!"

I rose from the sofa, unlocked the door, and asked him to enter.

"Thanks so much for taking the little monsters to Cade's folks, Huey," I said gratefully.

"Not a prob." He approached the couch and peered into the kits' little faces. "Wow! They're so cute, but do they bite?"

"No—at least, not yet," Cade replied.

We told Huey the names of the kits, then helped him load the animals and supplies into his car.

"Thanks again for doing this, Huey," Cade said.

"It's my pleasure, dude and dudette." Huey gave us his sweet, goofy grin and slowly reversed down the driveway.

As Huey drove away, I was relieved because this was one less thing to worry about. The kits were safe. But now what? The sense of foreboding still hung over my head because something horrific was headed my way. But I would do my best to hide it from Cade. Although, it would be easier said than done.

Chapter Nineteen

Cade and I settled into a routine, and he made sure I remained comfortable and at ease. I contacted Kogi about what transpired, and he stated that's probably why Cameron had been missing for a couple of days—to hire the hitter. Kogi also informed me he'd let me know if he discovered any new information.

Texting him back, I asked, "Kogi, do you have any idea why Cameron would want me dead? It doesn't make sense."

"I honestly can't say. But whatever the reason, stay vigilant, and I'll do what I can here."

I thanked him and put the phone away.

After two days of not hearing from Cade's brother, it was a relief when he finally showed up at our doorstep. His face gave nothing away as he walked through the door.

"I have some news," he said. "Most of it good, Hannah, so please remove that terrified look off your face, honey."

Smiling kindly at him, I kissed his cheek and we invited him to take a seat. Boone greeted Phoenix with muffled "aarfs" and offered him his squeaky pig toy. Phoenix patted Boone's head several times and sat down, pulling some folded papers from his breast pocket.

Looking at us gravely, Phoenix said, "My techs cracked the hitman's phone, and as far as we can tell, he didn't share your location with anyone else, Hannah. Plus, we know this perp's history, and he always worked alone and never shared a job with his competition. That's definitely in your favor."

"That *is* great news," I replied, then sighed. Cade rubbed my arm and I grinned weakly at him in response.

"However, that certainly doesn't mean another hitter wouldn't be hired once Martin McKay doesn't communicate back with whoever gave him the contract. But, it could buy us some time." Phoenix scratched his chin and pursed his lips.

"Okay, brother, what are you not telling us?" Cade asked.

Several seconds passed and Phoenix shifted in his seat. "I shouldn't be giving you this intelligence, but over the last eight months, we've had an undercover agent within the St. John ranks. However, we haven't heard from him for some time and are concerned he's been discovered and taken out. We're doing our best to investigate his whereabouts discreetly, but if he's still alive, we don't want to jeopardize his life if he's lying low. But, we're working on it."

"Do you have enough to take down the family and his nefarious cohorts?" Cade asked.

"That's just it. Our agent was supposed to get us the evidence we need, and we're also waiting on this as well. I wish the wheels could move faster, but we're doing our best." Phoenix stared at his feet for a moment, then stood up and faced us.

I stared at my hands, bit my lip, and shifted in my seat.

"Hannah, what's wrong?" Cade asked.

"Well, I might have some information on Trace's organization, but I'm not positive." The two men looked at me, waiting for me to continue. I stood up and wrung my hands as I cleared my throat. "Uh…before I ran away, I hacked Trace's business computer and downloaded a lot of data."

"That's fantastic, sweetheart!"

"Before you get too excited, it's all encrypted. I couldn't make heads or tails of any of it. But I have the two flash drives, Phoenix, if you want them."

"Definitely," Phoenix replied with a satisfied grin. "This could be the break we've been waiting for."

I retrieved the flash drives from my room and handed them to Cade's brother.

"Don't worry. I'll let both of you know when my team hacks through the encryption and extracts the data." Phoenix stood up and continued, "Hannah, you can return to your home. You'd never know there'd been a shooting or that a man had died. It's clean as a whistle—and before you protest, Cade, I'll have an agent keep an eye on her and the property. Will that make you happy?"

Cade returned his brother's gaze with narrowed eyes and gave him a slight nod. "This man better be good. You can vouch for him?"

"One hundred percent."

I stared from one brother to the other, wondering why no one spoke to me.

"Hey, remember me? This is my life, you know. It's my decision, and I trust your brother, Cade. I'm returning to my home and that's my final answer." I would've stomped my foot if I thought it wouldn't have been childish.

Cade grinned as he replied, "Okay, my little firecracker, we'll get you back home. But I'm moving back in too. Understood?"

I peered at him under my lashes, then answered in feigned exasperation, "If you must. But I have to say, it's torture living with you, Cade. Sheesh!"

Phoenix snickered as he exited the door.

Once we were alone, Cade pulled me close and whispered seductively into my ear, "I'm sure you'll find a way to put up with me, Hannah."

He kissed the side of my neck. I sighed as his touch made my toes curl again. "See what I mean? You're intolerable...."

RETURNING TO MY HOME BROUGHT ME JOY, YET A HINT OF DREAD. THE front door had been repaired, and the bullet holes in the attic were fixed. As

I inspected "the killing zone," there were no signs of blood—just as Phoenix had said. For some reason, though, I still walked around where the body had been, giving it a wide berth.

My phone from Kogi remained quiet and I took that as a good omen. But according to Cade's brother, time wasn't on my side. I had my weapon back and I decided to carry it with me. Cade knew and he never said a word about it.

Taking another walk in the woods was just what I needed, and Boone and Milo were also thrilled. They hopped and barked with joy when I put them on leashes. I took the usual route and came across Lois.

"Hey, neighbor!" she hollered. "I missed you. Are you okay, honey?"

"I'm fine, Lois. But thanks for asking."

We took our usual stroll down to the lake and sat on the driftwood. Boone and Milo played on the shoreline and chased the seagulls in a game of tag. The gentle lapping of the waves against the sand soothed my soul.

Nothing was said for several minutes while we enjoyed the sounds of the lake, the birds, and the gentle wind tickling the leaves on the trees.

"You know, honey, it'll all work out. You'll see." Lois squeezed my hand and I gave her a thankful smile.

"Will it, though? It seems like wherever I go, or whatever I do, mayhem follows."

"That's not true—though I'm sure it may seem that way to you. You're a good soul and God is looking out for you. Trust me, dear. And you have a good man at your side to protect and care for you—plus me, don't forget!"

I gave her a warm hug. "I know, you're right. I'll try to keep a positive attitude."

"That's my girl. We'll enjoy the beautiful day the Lord has made, and let us rejoice and be glad!" Lois chimed.

AFTER I RETURNED TO THE COTTAGE, CADE SUGGESTED WE TRY THE EQUINE therapy he'd mentioned earlier.

"Cade, really? I'm not comfortable with this idea—and is it safe—I mean, with someone out there trying to murder me?"

"Are you going to finagle your way out of getting help with your

PTSD, my dear?" He wiggled his eyebrows at me and kissed me soundly. "Honestly, we'll be fine. We have our trusted bodyguard, plus Mr. Ruger is strapped tightly to my hip."

I thought about it for a few minutes and reluctantly agreed. I donned a pair of comfortable jeans, a T-shirt, and sturdy shoes.

The stable was large but pristine and the horses looked terrifying. I stared wide-eyed at Cade and he squeezed my hand with reassurance. "Hannah, these horses are sweet and gentle. Trust me, hmm?"

A huge man and one smaller guy approached Cade and me. The two males traded fist bumps with Cade, and they gave each other a couple of slaps on the back.

Cade turned to me and said, "Hannah, these are my good buddies, Gator and Wilson. We've been good friends since our days in the Navy. Gator is the big galoot, and the handsome, skinny blonde guy is Wilson."

"I'm not skinny, you ugly monkey," Wilson replied with a grin and a wink. He was only a couple of inches shorter than the other two men. Although on the leaner side, he was well-muscled and handsome with curly blond hair, bright blue eyes, and a dimpled smile. "Hi, Hannah—it's a pleasure to meet you." He took my hand firmly and gave me a gentle hug.

The giant of a man stepped toward me, and I instinctively stumbled backward. Gator didn't seem to notice and pulled me into a bear hug. I could barely breathe. He set me away from him, and I looked up at the mountain of a man who resembled a cross between Dwayne Johnson and a young Arnold Schwarzenegger. Although his head was bald, he had a trim black goatee. Smiling politely, I stared questioningly at Cade.

"Hannah, we were in the Seals together. Gator may be big, but he's the best demo man in the business. And Wilson is our sniper, and he can take out a target at three-thousand yards," Cade said.

"That's three-thousand, four-hundred and twenty-two yards, my man," Wilson interjected, "but who's counting…."

The other two men rolled their eyes and I snickered.

Cade continued, "The three of us started this place to help other veterans and anyone else who may need help with past trauma and PTSD."

"This all belongs to you guys?" I said in shock and was duly impressed.

"It sure does. Now how about we get you started, little lady?" Gator asked.

I nodded and tightened my grip on Cade's hand. He squeezed it in return and gave me a reassuring smile. Nodding, Gator guided us to the arena, where two stable hands held a couple of horses. As we approached them, their massive size startled me. Cade gripped my hand again and led me forward.

"I can attest to the temperament of these two babies, Hannah," Cade said. "This horse, which is a Palomino mare, is called Sunshine. She's a gentle soul and loves to be sweet-talked." Cade walked me up to her head and I immediately stepped back. Cade gently pulled me forward again, and when I approached Sunshine, she lowered her long neck and butted me gently in the chest with her nose.

"See? She already likes you," Gator replied with a huge smile. "Stroke her muzzle, kiddo."

I did as he asked and a silly grin broke over my face. "This is so cool!" I whispered in response. The stable hand who held the horse guided me to stand closer to Sunshine's neck. The gentle giant softly breathed against my arm and simply stood close to me. I felt her warmth, which was comforting, and it surprised me that there was no smelly odor. It was a clean earthy smell and I found it quite pleasant.

Glancing at Cade, he stood with a huge brown and white horse named Cherokee, and Cade was already in the saddle. He grinned joyfully at me and was a natural with horses and riding.

"Do I have to do that?" I screeched, causing Sunshine to retreat a couple of steps.

"Not today or maybe never. It's all up to you, Hannah," Wilson replied.

"That's a relief." I approached the horse again, and she resumed her stance with her head against my chest.

Cade and his horse were already on the other side of the arena and he prodded Cherokee into a gentle trot.

I spent several minutes acclimating to being this close to such a large animal, and I asked the young stable hand if I could lead Sunshine around the arena. She handed me the rope, and when I gently pulled on the halter, the horse followed. Gator and Wilson told me to have a good time and would catch me later. Giving them both a wave and a smile, I returned my attention to the massive beast on the end of a terrifyingly thin rope.

"Look, Cade, I'm leading a horse!"

"That you are, sweetheart. Good job!"

For the next half hour, I stayed close to Sunshine and loved every moment. I brushed her soft coat, which soothed the sweet horse and me. When my time was about up, I wrapped my arms around her and held her close, inhaling her earthly, comforting scent. Staying that way for several minutes, I let myself relax, and when I finally pulled away, I discovered tears on my face. I quietly thanked the young stable hand, quickly turned away, and shuffled toward the exit. Once I reached the outside, I couldn't stop crying.

Warm arms surrounded me and I smelled Cade's spicy aftershave. Burying my face in his shirt, I let the tears flow. He murmured comforting words and stroked my back as I released all the frustration, fear, and anger that had been pent up inside me for so long.

Several minutes later, I backed away, and Cade handed me some tissues.

I blubbered, "I'm s-s-sorry. I don't know what h-happened to me."

"Hannah, that's what this therapy is for—although I've never seen it work that fast before."

"When can we come back?" I asked with a coy smile.

"Whenever you want to, darlin'. Whenever you want."

THAT EVENING, CADE INSISTED WE GO ON ANOTHER DATE. WE ONLY HAD one so far, and it was time for a "little romance," Cade said with a frisky grin.

I donned a cute cocktail dress I'd recently purchased and piled on the makeup and hairspray. Cade met me downstairs, looking incredibly handsome in his dark, tailored suit. His hair glistened from his recent shower and he smelled heavenly. I groaned when he kissed me hello, and I melted into his strong yet gentle embrace.

"I could stay like this all day, Cade," I said into his jacket, snuggling closer.

"Ahem...I don't think that would be a good idea, Hannah," Once I realized what he meant, I slowly eased away with a sigh, grinned like a Cheshire cat, and batted my eyelashes at him.

I answered Cade in a robust southern belle accent. "I don't have a clue what you mean, sir. I'm simply an innocent lady with no experience with the likes of men," I glanced a bashful look at Cade, and the expression on his face was priceless. A loud snort escaped my lips and it turned into gales of laughter.

"You're such a tease!" he retorted, then joined in with a couple of loud guffaws. After giving me a quick kiss, he escorted me to the driveway. "We're taking your car because I want to drive that monster of a 442 engine."

I handed him my keys and reminded him we had to say the St. Michael prayer before leaving the driveway. When we finished the chant, we drove to the Italian restaurant he had taken me to on our first date. Cade's masculine appreciation of my souped-up vehicle didn't go unnoticed as we drove through town and into the parking lot. He revved the engine several times at the traffic lights and then when he parked the car.

I mumbled, "Show-off," and he grinned with satisfaction.

The meal was exquisite and the dessert, heavenly. I could have purred while I savored the tiramisu. When I looked up, Cade focused on my mouth as if mesmerized. His sensual stare caused me to choke on the delicious confection.

When I could finally speak, I said, "Cade, stop looking at me like that —it makes me feel...well, you know!" I tried to keep my voice down so the other diners wouldn't hear my words, but my utterances sounded more like a hyped-up chipmunk who'd inhaled helium.

Cade couldn't contain himself and chortled with gales of laughter at my squeaky response. So much for not disturbing the other patrons in the restaurant. Everyone stared at the two of us, but when I gazed at their faces, they were only grinning because of Cade's infectious guffaws.

When he finished laughing, he wiped the tears from his eyes and said, "Sweetheart, you do have a way of tickling my funny bone—as well as affecting other parts of my anatomy."

"Oh—stop!" I rolled my eyes at him but still had to stifle a giggle.

After our meal, we returned to the cottage, went to the deck, and sat gazing at the lake. The moon was full, the stars were bright, and the night sounds of the common loons echoed their music across the water. The humid night air was scented with roses, freshly cut grass, and for some reason, a hint of mint.

"Why do I smell peppermint?" I asked Cade, delicately sniffing around his person, thinking it came from him.

"Well, I do declare, darlin', are you actually sniffing me?" he asked indignantly.

"Sorry."

He chuckled and said, "Actually, a farmer a few miles down the road grows mint. Even though this isn't the best area for growing the herb, the guy insists on planting it yearly. On humid nights like this, it can be quite pungent. It's even stronger when it's harvest time."

"Really? It smells nice." I inhaled another large, exaggerated whiff, and a small bug flew up my nose. Standing up quickly, I jumped up and down, trying to dislodge the nasty thing from my nostril.

"What on earth are you doing?" he asked as he chuckled at my antics.

"A…bug…went up my…nose!"

"Oh, is that all?"

"Argh!" I complained and stomped into the cottage to grab a tissue to remove the offending critter.

Cade followed me into the house and I stormed into the bathroom and slammed the door. A few minutes later, I casually strolled back into the kitchen where Cade sat at the island.

"You okay, my little beastie snorter?" he asked with a silly grin.

"Bite me!" I said a little snidely as I attempted to hide a smirk.

"Just say when, beautiful."

"You're incorrigible," I snickered and plopped onto the seat beside him.

Cade reached up and tucked a stray lock of hair behind my ear. His eyes grew dark with sensual awareness and he caressed my cheek with his fingers. I closed my eyes and enjoyed the simple stroke of his hand. It was an innocent touch, but it invoked an intense connection with this incredible man.

When he pulled his hand away, I felt bereft and opened my eyes to return his gaze. This gorgeous man reached up again, taking my chin into his hand, and he touched his lips to mine. I couldn't help myself as I buried my hands in his thick, silky hair and deepened the kiss. We both moaned as Cade pulled me onto his lap, and all sensibility left me. My conscious thoughts were a thing of the past, and I could only feel this incredible connection between us.

I thought I heard a strange noise—like growling. Then I felt a couple of hard taps on the right side of my head. Cade swiftly pulled his mouth away from mine and mumbled a curse. Since I was sitting on his lap, I could feel Cade's leg being jerked back and forth. When I looked down, Boone had Cade's pant leg gripped firmly in his teeth. The little dog pulled viciously at his trousers as if his life depended on it. I moved back to my seat and watched the incredible scene unfold before me.

"Boone—bad dog!" Cade yelled in reprimand, but luckily, Boone had already released his pant leg. "What in the Sam Hill is wrong with him?" Cade asked in confusion. "I'm not wearing a red cap, for goodness sake!"

"I'm sorry, Cade. I don't know what got into him. Just ignore Boone and kiss me again, handsome."

Cade leaned in and kissed me deeply once more.

It happened again—*whap, whap*! This time, something slapped my cheek. I turned to investigate what had been smacking me in the head. A loud howl erupted from the island countertop. Jig sat on his big, furry butt directly before me, only a few inches away. His bright green eyes glared back at me with disbelief and censure. He'd been hitting me with his gigantic paws—and luckily for me, he hadn't used his razor-sharp claws. Once I acknowledged Jig's presence, he turned his back to me, raised his huge fluffy tail, jumped off the counter, and strutted away.

I stroked my face and contemplated why these two generally well-adjusted animals would attack us.

Turning back to Cade, I said, "Why did they do that?"

"I haven't a clue," he replied, his eyebrows knitted together in concentration.

After we sat there for a few minutes, realization dawned on both of us simultaneously.

"You don't think…." I trailed off, staring at him in wonder.

"That God used Jig and Boone to stop us from doing the nasty?" Cade asked deviously, pretending to stroke his imaginary, dastardly deed mustache.

We both laughed and said at the same time, "Nah!!"

Chapter Twenty

The next day, I returned to my writing. But after several minutes of typing, I heard a *ding* from the phone Kogi had given me. A new text blinked at me, and I dreaded reading the message.

"Hannah, something's going on with Cameron. He appears to be gathering some of his men and preparing for travel. The man I hired said the St. John's jet has been fueled and a flight plan filed. Their destination is Michigan. One other odd thing is they show six passengers on the manifest, but we've only seen five of them, plus the two crew members. Who's the sixth passenger? We don't know, and they're leaving after dark the day after tomorrow. Stay safe."

My hands shook as I responded to his text. I thanked him and said I'd keep in touch.

I have to tell Cade.

I found him working outside with Gus as they put the final touches on the flower garden in the newly fenced-in side yard.

"Cade...." He looked up from joking with Gus, and once he saw the look on my face, he stood, discarded his gloves, and strode urgently toward me.

"Hannah, what is it?"

"They're coming for me."

Gus's head popped up and he glanced in our direction. He kept digging in the soil but peeked under his lashes as he listened to our conversation.

"Kogi—the man I told you about—he texted me and said Trace's brother and five other people will be leaving tomorrow night and are coming to Michigan. He said the four others in the group he knows work for Cameron, but he has no clue as to the identity of the sixth person. Cade, they're coming to kill me."

He pulled me close and said, "Don't worry. We've got you covered, honey. Let's go into the house and we'll contact Phoenix. Gus, I know you heard it all, so you might as well join us inside." Gus stood and followed us into the cottage, and we sat at the kitchen table. Cade called his brother.

My hands wouldn't stop shaking, and to my surprise, Gus took them in his and gave them a comforting squeeze. I sent him a grateful smile and continued to hang on to him.

After several minutes, Cade hung up and asked me to contact Kogi again. "Ask him if he has names and photos of all the people coming on that plane. We need to know." I nodded and ran up the stairs to contact Kogi. Returning to the kitchen, I found Cade back on his cell, talking to a couple of people on a conference call.

"Thanks, good buddies. I'll see you then." He disconnected the call and faced Gus. "Gus, you can't tell anyone what you heard here today. The FBI is aware of the threat on Hannah's life and will assist in protecting her. Do I have your word you won't say anything to anyone?"

Gus returned our gaze with a stoic expression and said nothing for several moments, but then spoke up, "I won't say a word, but I can help. You know I'm a veteran too, and even though I'm old, I'm still an excellent shot."

Cade rubbed his jaw, obviously trying to decide how to politely turn the old man down on his offer.

"I need to do this, Cade. I feel it in my bones," Gus replied firmly.

"Okay—but you have to follow whatever orders you're given without question," Cade said.

Gus nodded in compliance and remained seated at the table.

"Hannah, my Seal team buddies you met at the stables are on their way over. We'll need their help and they're the best at what they do. Phoenix is assembling his team and will arrive shortly. A plan will be put into place to protect you. Please pack a bag and we'll move you somewhere safe. Understood?" Cade stared into my eyes, expecting me to follow his order.

"No. I need to stay—I'm not running anymore. It ends here." Standing firm, I held my ground against Cade and whatever he might say to try and change my decision.

"Hannah—"

"I mean it, Cade."

"No!"

Cade angrily paced the kitchen. The dogs dodged back and forth, attempting to stay out from under his feet. His phone vibrated, and he answered curtly. "Cade here...Oh, hello, Julian. I'm busy right now, can I call you back later?... No...no, sure. Go ahead and tell me what's so important." A few minutes passed and Cade's face turned ashen. "But, are you sure?... I see. Okay... No, I understand. Thanks, Julian." He disconnected the call and sat down hard on one of the kitchen chairs. Cade stared blankly out the window with a faraway look in his eyes.

"Cade, what did your nephew say?" I asked.

He didn't respond, so I repeated the question.

After several more moments, he finally turned to look at me. "Julian said—and I quote—'Hannah must be in the house when the bad guys come.'"

"Really?" Both Gus and I replied at the same time.

"Yeah."

"Okay then, so what's the plan?" Gus asked.

Cade stood and replied, "Once my brother and friends arrive, that's what we're going to discuss. Hannah, have you heard back from Kogi?"

Glancing down at the phone in my hand, I answered, "No, not yet. He said it might take a couple of hours to get the intel. But he'll get it to us—you can count on him."

"Good. I'm going to call my dad to come and pick up the dogs and Jig. They would only get in the way or get killed—we need them safe," Cade said.

I agreed and boxed up some food and toys for the animals.

Cade's friends showed up, and they hugged me again, and I told them

163

how much I appreciated their assistance. Phoenix and his team arrived a few minutes later. We sat down and hashed out several ideas for handling this situation. My phone buzzed from Kogi. He supplied photographs and matching names—at least of Cameron and four other people—three men and one woman. I recognized them from Trace's crew. They were bad news.

Kogi still didn't have any information on the sixth person coming in on the flight. "I don't get it," I squawked at no one in particular while my fingers rubbed my forehead in frustration. "I mean, what's the big secret?"

Phoenix shook his head, "I haven't a clue either. All we can do is prepare and be ready for anything. My team's checking on all incoming flights, especially private airstrips in this area, and we'll widen our search from there. In the meantime, we must prepare the property and have our strategy in place. Let's get started."

After a couple of hours, I found their expertise and military training mindboggling, including what they devised to protect me and themselves.

After serving the men a hearty lunch, everyone departed to prepare for the upcoming mission. Cade stayed behind and was back on his phone. He ordered some lumber, nails, and several things I didn't recognize, and it would be delivered within the hour.

Cade's dad arrived and picked up the animals. Although it was sad to see them leave, I knew it was necessary to keep them safe. Giving both dogs and the cat kisses, I released them into Frank Copano's care. Frank also gave us both hugs.

Even though he didn't know the entire story of what was about to happen, he said, "Whatever you're both having to face, the entire family will pray for you." We watched as they drove away, and my heart felt heavy. Arms encircled me from behind and I settled back into Cade's warmth.

He whispered into my ear, "God's on our side, honey, and he's given us people who are the best at what they do. Even old Gus. He retired from the Marines after thirty years of service. Even though he may be long in the tooth, he's far from weak and frail. He's a tough old bird—you'll see."

"I know. It's just—I don't want anyone hurt because of me."

"We'll do our best so that doesn't happen. All we can do at the moment is wait for the intel as to which airport they'll be using and the time of their arrival. Once the supplies are delivered, we'll have a lot of work to do."

THE NEXT TWENTY-FOUR HOURS KEPT US BUSY. CADE AND HIS CREW boarded up most of the windows in the house, allowing just enough room between the slats for someone to see outside. Wilson dug holes in the ground around the perimeter as well, and I didn't ask what they were for— although I had an idea and found it frightening.

We discovered where their plane would be landing, and it was a private airstrip about an hour from my cottage. Cade asked Huey to call in when their jet landed but ordered him to stay far away from Cameron and his men. According to our estimation, they should arrive at my cabin around 5:00 a.m. at the earliest.

We all wore dark camouflage clothing, and when Gator, Cade, Wilson, and Phoenix walked into my kitchen, they looked like they should be in an episode of one of the "Rambo" movies. Their skin was covered in paint, and they appeared ready to take out an enemy encampment. Phoenix placed several men in strategic vantage points outside the cottage and around the property.

Cade turned to me and said, "Hannah, your job is to stay in the attic behind the barricade we built. If anyone comes through the hatch door, fire until the person is dead. We'll communicate through these earbuds, so if one of us comes to the third floor, we'll announce ourselves first. Got it?"

I nodded as Cade put a small communication bud into my ear and stuffed the battery pack into one of my pockets. He pulled my handgun from the holster on my hip, double-checked the clip, and made sure a bullet was already in the chamber. Returning the gun, he then addressed Gus.

"You, my man, will remain on the second floor with two FBI agents. Please do your best to keep your head down. We all have our night vision goggles, and I assume they'll also be wearing them. When they arrive, we know they'll cut the power before attempting to enter the property. That's what we would do. I've disconnected the on-demand generator because the darkness would also be to our advantage.

"Whatever happens, Hannah, do *not* leave the attic until we give you the all-clear. The windows are bulletproof glass, but it won't stop a grenade, so stay out of sight. Do you understand?" Cade threw me another hard look and I nodded once more. He pulled me into a bear hug and when he stepped back, he lovingly caressed my face. I blinked back the tears and quickly turned away.

After composing myself, I said, "I want all of you to know how much I appreciate you putting your lives on the line for me, and I don't understand why you'd do this for a stranger. But thank you." I gave them all warm embraces and wiped the tears from my eyes again. Everyone hugged me back and mumbled, "you're welcome."

"Okay, let's get a few bites of food. I know it's difficult to eat under the circumstances, but we'll need all the energy we can get when the time arrives," Cade replied.

We sat down to dinner and once Cade said a prayer of thanks and protection, we ate in silence. I did my best to shove the food into my mouth, but every bite was tasteless and sat like lead in my belly.

When it was time, I went up to the attic and took my place behind a low, three-walled area that Cade and his friends had built for me. The construction came from boilerplate carbon steel, and it was approximately three feet high and three feet wide and attached to the floor with steel brackets. A notch was cut out so as I knelt behind the wall, I could peek through the opening. It was just large enough for me to rest the barrel of my weapon through it, plus I could see the hatch perfectly. I chanted the St. Michael prayer and asked him to protect me and all the good people trying to keep me safe.

A sense of *déjà vu* spiraled through me—and of course, I'd done this before. *Here we go again, Hannah. You're in another shootout!* I rolled my eyes at my ludicrous thoughts and forced myself to concentrate on the task at hand.

As I checked my watch, it was approaching 4:52 a.m. My stomach started to churn and I searched for a place to throw up. I found a container and vomited.

"Dang it," I muttered.

"Hannah, are you alright?" Cade's voice whispered through my earbud.

"Uh—yeah. I just lost my dinner—nothing serious." A few sympathetic comments were made, and thankfully, they didn't laugh.

"That's a normal reaction, kiddo. You'll be fine," Gator replied in his gruff, deep voice.

Click. The attic and the entire house went black, including the mercury flood lights by the barn.

"Heads up, team," Wilson whispered.

"Let's get this party started," Cade answered back.

The loudest noise was the *thump-thump-thump* of my heart as it raced in my chest. I attempted to slow my breathing as I felt lightheaded. *In through my nose, out through my mouth.* Keeping the mantra going, my frantic respiration and brisk banging in my chest began to calm.

Boom! It was an explosion.

Dang! I guess I'd been correct about Gator planting explosives on the property. I heard a deep yell but didn't recognize the voice—thank goodness. My gun shook slightly in my hands as I kept it trained on the hatch door through the small notch in my protective metal wall.

Rapid and loud gunfire echoed outside the window to my right, and I could see the flashes reflected into the night sky. *Thump, thump.* That had to be a handgun with a suppressor. There were pings as a few stray bullets hit one of the attic windows. Thank goodness for the bulletproof glass.

"Cade?"

Silence.

"Cade?" I whispered once more.

"I'm here, but I can't talk. I'm on the trail of a hostile—there are so many of them! Just stay where you are…." His breathless response told me he must have been running.

Several more shots could be heard, and the front and back doors were knocked down with loud, reverberating bangs. Vomit entered my throat and I swallowed hard to keep it down.

More gunfire boomed from the lower floors. My ears closed off, and I swallowed hard to restore my hearing. Unfortunately, it didn't help much.

Boom! Boom! The house vibrated from the cacophony of the blasts. My team's voices echoed in my ear, and I couldn't decipher their words. They weren't speaking to me, but to each other, and used military jargon, so I didn't understand them anyway. More shots went off outside and two more down below me.

Pounding footsteps echoed from downstairs as the intruders searched the lower floors to find me. My hands shook harder and I struggled again with my breathing. *In through my nose, out through my mouth.*

The attic hatch door shot open and I ducked as splinters of wood and metal flew around the room. I fired my weapon toward the opening as a reflex action.

Crap!

Chapter Twenty-One

Automatic weapon fire came through the top of the hatch. My instant response was to duck low and cover my head. However, I still gripped my weapon, and after the deafening noise stopped, I took a quick peek through the slot.

One man with a helmeted head appeared above the opening, and he scanned the room with his rifle, ready to shoot at anything that moved. His survey stopped when he spotted me staring at him from behind the metal barricade. He spoke into a radio strapped to his chest without altering his gaze. "The target is up here, boss." I couldn't hear the response, but I was sure it was Cameron at the other end of the conversation.

Raising my gun, I rested it back into the slot. I thought about shooting him, but he wore full armor. My only option was to either hit him in the arm or wait until he completely entered the room so I could shoot him in the thigh.

There was a loud click and the lights came on. I removed the night goggles and the man at the hatch did as well.

"I wouldn't advise trying to shoot me, girlie. You're heavily out-gunned," he replied arrogantly as he read my mind. *Dang, I wished my ears would stop ringing!*

"Please don't hurt me...." I tried being the helpless female again, hoping he'd think he had the upper hand and make a careless move. It worked.

The shooter climbed up into the attic and stood beside the opening. Through my muffled hearing, I detected footsteps on the stairs, and another person appeared—who I assumed was a woman because of her lighter build. She also wore full armor.

Dang it! I fired a shot and caught the first man in the leg. He roared in anger and fired back. The bullet pinged off the metal and landed in the drywall beside his head.

"Stop firing, you imbecile! I want her alive!" Cameron's voice shouted from below the hatch. "Restrain her!"

Even though I shot the man in the leg, he attempted to hobble toward me, and the woman pointed her pistol at me. Another man entered the room from below, but it wasn't Cameron. I now had three shooters who had their guns aimed in my direction.

What do I do now? I shook in terror as they surrounded me. Taking the offensive, I fired a couple more shots, attempting to hit any of the intruders, but they moved too fast.

Then something occurred to me. "St. Michael!" I yelled. "Please come to my aid!"

The room came alive with static electricity. My hair actually crackled when I turned my head to gaze through the hole in my protective wall. I even smelled ozone in the room. A strange *whoomp, whoomp* sound echoed around me. What on earth caused that bizarre noise?

Peeking through the hole once more, the man closest to me had terror in his eyes. He stopped in mid-stride and froze in place. "No!" he screamed. Even though my vantage point was limited, I witnessed the man being lifted from the floor and thrown through the ceiling and out the roof. Pieces of drywall, insulation, wood, and shingles fell through the gaping hole and littered the attic floor.

Several shots were fired again, although they weren't aimed at me but toward someone or something else. I couldn't hide anymore—I had to see what was happening.

I heard the woman shooter scream as my head popped around the side of the metal wall. An enormous entity blocked my view of the female hitter. Although I could only see the back of this being, I spotted long, wavy auburn hair and a massively strong, muscular body. The armor covering his torso flashed with iridescent silver and reflected constant movement and color. It seemed to have a life of its own. My eyes grew wide when I discovered the giant being standing in my attic was St. Michael!

Shrieking in terror, the woman fired several more shots at the being. The archangel only laughed at her pitiful attempts to kill him. St. Michael picked her up using one massive arm, then moved over to the last shooter in the room. This third man shrank back in terror and curled into a ball below one of the attic windows.

The room continued to crackle with some unknown electricity as St. Michael picked up the cowering man in his other arm and tossed them like two footballs out of the bulletproof window. After these criminals' unexpected flight through the glass, the night air blew into the room, and the drapes swayed and shimmied in the breeze.

I stood in shock beside my protective metal wall, stunned at the spectacle before me. St. Michael turned in my direction and I cowered down in fear.

"Return my gaze, child," he commanded. He had a deep voice and the resonance of it echoed through to my bones. I never saw his lips move, but I heard every word clearly and distinctly.

Peering upwards through my lashes, the archangel before me had a stare that could not be denied. I looked directly at him. The beauty of his face made me catch my breath, and his greenish-gold eyes flashed with knowledge, kindness, ruthlessness, cunning, and intense love.

St. Michael spoke to me again. "Return to your metal shelter. What happens next is your destiny, but trust in God, as He is always with you, child. What follows now is what is meant to be."

I smiled shyly and was about to thank him, but the room flashed with vibration and light, and the giant archangel vanished. The smell of ozone still filled the air, and the room was in shambles—obviously, something miraculous and violent had happened here. I did as he instructed and returned to hide behind my shelter.

"Rockwell, answer me! What the hell is going on up there?" Cameron's voice yelled up the stairs.

I answered back, "They're gone. If you want me, Cameron, you'll have to come and get me yourself."

Several moments passed before he answered. "Serena—or should I call you Hannah? Nah—you'll always be Serena to me. You'd better not shoot again or you'll hit this old man who was down on the lower level to protect you. Give up, little girl. You won't get away this time."

Gus's head popped through the opening. He carried his arms above his head in surrender and his face was ashen and filled with pain.

What did they do to him?

I whispered to my team, "They're in the attic and using Gus as a shield." My voice wasn't recognizable to my ears as it shook with terror. I focused on Gus's pained expression. Someone shoved him from below and I fumed with anger. Gus brought one hand down and pulled it to his chest in pain.

Oh Gus, no—it's your heart?

"Hurry up, guys! I think Gus is having a heart attack—he looks bad." I whispered. Staying in place, I waited for them to make the next move.

"Hannah, we're coming," Cade replied.

Keeping my weapon trained on the hatch, Gus was shoved through the door and Cameron stayed firmly behind him. I wasn't a good enough shot to hit Cameron behind the poor old man.

"Put your weapon down, Serena."

"No way, Cameron. That's not going to happen," I replied, keeping my tone steady and firm. My blood boiled at what Cameron had done to Gus, and the anger helped to steady my gun hand.

The two men now stood in the attic and I didn't know what to do.

Cameron stared in disbelief at the destruction of the room. He scanned every inch, taking in the broken window, the hole in the roof, and the three missing hired hands.

"Good grief—what the hell happened here, Serena? Hmmm?" Cameron asked in surprise. I said nothing, and he continued, "No matter, get out here, girl!" He pushed his weapon harder into Gus's skull.

"Not in a million years," I replied.

Bang! A single shot echoed through the attic. I assumed Cameron had shot Gus in the head, but the poor old man had been hit in the thigh instead. Gus howled and tried to grab his injury, but Cameron held him fast. I stared in disbelief because the shot had been fired from someone below the hatch door, not from Cameron.

"Drop your gun, or next time, it'll be a lethal wound," Cameron warned.

I couldn't let this happen to Gus. Dropping my weapon, I stood up, although the barricade still hid most of my body.

Cameron turned to look down toward the stairs and said, "Come on up. She's dropped her weapon."

As I glanced toward the hatch, a man's head appeared while he slowly climbed through the opening.

"Hey, baby, did you miss me?" I gasped as Trace stood before me—the husband I thought I'd accidentally killed at the bluffs.

"You're alive…." I said in disbelief.

"Yeah, ain't that a hoot?" Trace sneered in satisfaction, then said, "You thought you killed me, but when you shoved me over the cliff, I landed onto a ledge. It took me the entire night to climb out of that hellhole, and with broken ribs and a concussion too. You did that to me, you filthy cow."

He moved forward and pulled me from behind the wall. After shoving me down to the floor, he aimed his weapon at my head. "You've been nothing but a thorn in my side since we met, Serena, and it's now over."

I quickly raised my left hand, which held my small, two-shot, derringer-style, 9 mm handgun. But I wasn't fast enough.

Everything happened in an instant. *Bang—bang—bang!* I jumped in reaction, assuming I'd been shot. When I glanced up, my husband had fallen to the ground and was now lying on his side. His eyes stared life-lessly at me, and I turned to find Cameron holding the smoking gun that had killed his brother. He shoved Gus away from him, and the poor old man sat down hard on the floor beside me. Gus applied pressure to the wound in his leg. More gunshots sounded from outside, and I heard yelling and additional weapons being discharged from down below.

Cameron jumped in front of me, and before I could react, he kicked the small pistol from my hand. I stood to face him. "It's my empire now," he said. "I wish you'd have killed him the first time, Serena. It would have made my life so much easier. We had to go through this charade because Trace wanted to be the one to kill you without you knowing he was still alive. My stupid brother always likes a show and makes everyone play along. But that's finally over."

Cameron traced my jawline with the barrel of his gun and said, "I'm sorry you still have to die, my dear. You know too much, and I know you stole the intel from Trace's computer that implicates me, and him. What did you do with the evidence, Serena? Hmmm?"

I backed up as far as possible but couldn't move any farther as the wall impeded my retreat. As I shifted my eyes to the right, I also spotted Gus struggling to stand. To my surprise, he grabbed my first pistol from the floor. But Cameron spotted him and shot Gus in the chest before the old man could fire. I screamed and ran to Gus. The smell of gunpowder and blood permeated the air.

"You're positively evil—just like your slimy brother!" Kneeling, I did my best to administer first-aid to Gus but couldn't staunch the bleeding. It gushed from his chest, and I knew it was a fatal wound. If the heart attack wouldn't kill him, the gunshot would. Cameron stood directly to my left, and I knew I couldn't reach the weapon Gus had dropped. But Cameron had made a fatal error as he turned toward the noise from the open hatch. He stood in the precise spot, at the perfect angle. I quickly kicked out my left leg, hitting Cameron behind the knees, and he lost his footing, dropping hard to the floor. The gun flew out of his hand, and I heard it clang as it bounced down the stairwell. I jumped on Cameron's back, locking my arms around him in a lethal choke hold. Tightening my grip, he struggled desperately to buck me off, but Kogi had trained me well.

I heard more noise from the doorway, but my anger kept my arms clamped around Gus's murderer.

"Hannah..." I only had one goal in mind, and it took several moments before I could hear Cade's voice whispering my name. "Hannah, honey. You have to let him go." A gentle hand touched my shoulder and I reluctantly released my grip. Cameron collapsed onto the floor, unconscious. I sat down hard on my butt, but when I saw Gus, I scampered over to him.

Wilson appeared and did his best to administer to the old guy. He kept pressure on the wound, but when Wilson returned my gaze, he shook his head in resignation. Gus had lost too much blood.

"Gus…." I begged with a shaky voice. Stroking his balding head in comfort, I tried to smile, and he looked at me with glazed and apologetic eyes.

"It's alright, Hannah. I wish I could have done more for you, but I never expected my ticker to give out on me, which gave those imbeciles… the edge. I'm…so…sorry." Gus's voice gasped as he struggled to breathe and gripped my hands. "Hannah…I also want you to know…that I'm sorry for treating you…so badly. It's just when I discovered you moved into this cottage…I saw red." He trailed off, trying to catch his breath. I held tighter to his cold hands as he continued his story. "I loved that beautiful woman with my whole heart, and I let my stubbornness ruin the best thing I ever had with my wonderful Margie. Do you think…she forgave me before she died, Hannah?"

His eyes stared pleadingly into mine and I didn't know how to answer. I went with sheer instinct and told him what he needed to hear. "Of course she did, Gus. She loved you, and that trumps everything. From what you said, you two had something special, so I know she forgave you. Come on, Gus, you better fight to live, old man!" I demanded, begging him to hang on.

He smiled and said, "No. If she forgave me, then I want to join Margie. The love of my life is waiting and it's time for me…to leave this world, Hannah. Don't you dare blame yourself for this. What happened here…was meant to be." Gus stared off somewhere over my shoulder. A sweet smile lit up his face, and he exclaimed with joy, using his last dying breath, "Margie!" and his eyes closed in finality.

"Gus!" I yelled, trying to shake him back to life as I ignored the tears running down my face.

"Hannah, he's gone. Let him be, sweetheart," Cade murmured into my ear. He took me into his arms and held me close. I felt Cade's body shudder in mourning as he cried for the loss of his dear friend.

After several minutes, my mind began to focus again, making me jerk backward, and I demanded, "Is everyone else on our team alright?" Looking around me, I saw Gator and Wilson watching me from across the room. They were a muddy mess and scratched up, but seemed fine. They moved over to Gus and covered his body with their jackets.

"We're good, kiddo," Gator replied in sorrow.

I glanced at Cade and caressed his painted and muddy face. "You too?" I asked.

"We're all fine," he replied. "But I'm sorry it took us so long to get to you. Unbeknownst to us, Cameron and Trace hired additional help here in Michigan. We had no clue, so we were up against many more men instead of merely six. But we kicked their butts—with the help of someone miraculous. You should have seen him, Hannah! He had to have been sent from God." His white smile gleamed brightly against his sooty, dark face. Tears still glimmered in his eyes as he glanced back at poor Gus.

I spoke up quickly, "You saw St. Michael? He's the one who took care of the first three shooters who entered the attic. It was astounding."

Cade looked around the room as well as up toward the ceiling. "He did all this?"

"Yes. Did you get to see what he looked like, Cade?" I asked.

"We all did, Hannah," Wilson replied. Their stunned expressions told the story of whom they'd seen.

More footsteps came up the stairs and Phoenix announced himself. The poor guy also appeared worse for wear but not harmed. Looking around the room, Phoenix spotted the two brothers on the floor, as well as poor Gus. A flicker of regret and pain passed over his face, but he said, "Is everyone else okay in here?"

Cade spoke up, "We lost Gus, but the rest of us are fine. How about your team?"

"A few bumps and bruises, but we're good." Phoenix looked at me, then down at Trace's body. "Hannah, I guess you didn't kill him a few months ago. Did you just shoot him now?"

"It wasn't me. Cameron actually shot him." At that moment, Cameron came to and rubbed his badly bruised neck.

"Did he now?" Phoenix asked as two of his agents pulled Cameron to his feet, cuffed his hands behind his back, and ushered him downstairs. A couple more of Phoenix's men came into the attic, collected the weapons, and told us to go downstairs to the living room. I gladly followed his order so I wouldn't have to look at the two horrific dead bodies. I glanced back one last time at Gus, but Cade took my arm and led me to the stairs.

Phoenix scratched his head in confusion and said, "Did I imagine it, or did I see a gigantic, red-haired—"

"You did!" we all answered at the same time.

Phoenix made a sign of the cross and kissed an imaginary rosary. "My Lord in Heaven. Thank you for your protection," he whispered.

"By the way, Hannah," Cade interjected, "St. Michael helped us enter the house. Cameron's men tried to get in behind Cameron and Trace, but for some reason, they couldn't break through any of the doorways. It was the darndest thing. As we moved in, these poor idiots tried everything to get inside to protect their bosses, but no matter what they did, they couldn't walk through the doorways. They tried entering at a dead run but were bounced back as if they had hit a giant rubber band. That's when we saw St. Michael, and he took them out with one swipe of his gigantic arm. Talk about mind-blowing! I think that archangel had been toying with his prey —it was hilarious!"

Gator rumbled with laughter and added, "When we approached the doorway, we didn't know if we could get in, but we simply walked through. If it wasn't for him, it would have taken us much longer to get in here—if at all."

I stared at him in shock. No one would ever believe what happened here—it had to be a miracle.

Cade requested that we give thanks to God, and St. Michael and I avidly agreed.

A couple of hours later, we assembled downstairs in the kitchen while the FBI team did their work.

As it turned out, Trace and Cameron brought thirty people with them. Some came in on another flight and the rest were hired locally.

"That certainly explains why we were overrun," I replied in disbelief.

Cade said, "They weren't taking any chances on your survival, Hannah. We have to assume once their first hitman was killed, they knew someone was watching over you."

"I'm so sorry, Hannah, that we didn't do enough to protect you," Phoenix apologized. "No one should have made it into the house, much less up to the third floor. It's our fault for underestimating the number of shooters involved or the kind of weapons they brought with them."

I smiled and replied, "That's okay. None of us expected so many bad guys. Are your people okay, Phoenix?"

"A few of my people were hit inside the house, but nothing fatal. Luckily, their vests took the brunt of the bullets. They'll survive."

"Praise the Lord," Gator replied.

"Amen to that, brother," Cade murmured with a smile.

Phoenix spoke again, "By the way, Hannah, Gus did a great job for being an eighty-four-year-old Marine veteran. He took out two of the perps before he had his heart attack. That's when they grabbed him and shoved him up the stairwell. We're very proud of that man."

Just as he spoke about Gus, two EMTs carried his body down the stairs on a gurney. I felt my eyes tear up again and Cade pulled me close.

"It's okay, sweetheart," he murmured in consolation.

Another couple of men carried down the second body from the upper floors. I spotted my deceased husband. Surprisingly, I felt nothing at seeing him dead on a gurney.

Angrily brushing the tears away, I said to everyone, "Thank you for everything you did to protect me. I'm sure this will be the talk of the town for a while."

"I'm sure you're right about that, kiddo," Wilson said with a grin. "But be proud of yourself. You took down a couple of lethal crime bosses."

"That she did!" Phoenix replied. "On that note, we deciphered the data from the flash drives you gave us, Hannah. It contains everything we need to take down the entire town and then some. It also provided the intel as to what happened to our undercover agent. I'm sorry to say they killed him." A sorrowful look entered his eyes, and he bowed his head for a moment to compose himself.

After a few breaths, Phoenix looked at me again and said, "You did a great job." He gave me a quick hug. "My team will be here for a couple of days compiling evidence, and the coroner will arrive in a few minutes to collect the bodies. You two will have to move back to Cade's home for a bit."

Gator and Wilson left to return home, as it was now after dawn.

The sheriff arrived because of the noise complaints from several of my neighbors. Phoenix took him aside and explained everything to his satisfaction. Sheriff Mac was kind and told me if I ever needed help, he'd always be here for me. I gave him a pleased smile and thanked him kindly.

Cade and I packed our bags and returned to his place. I missed the dogs and Jig, but all I could think about taking a shower and getting some sleep.

Chapter Twenty-Two

A week passed, and we could return to the cozy cottage on the lake. Cade and I inspected the house and the grounds, and it was as if that terrible night had never happened. I dreaded going into the attic, but Cade insisted. A new hatch door replaced the bullet-filled one, which was now left open.

When I entered the space, the temporary steel walls were gone, the hole in the roof had been fixed, and the room was repainted a light, cheery yellow. Someone placed a gigantic vase of bright, fragrant flowers in the location where Gus had died. It seemed fitting. He loved posies and the thoughtful tribute warmed my heart.

"Cade...what a great idea. He would have loved this," I replied in a choked voice.

"I thought so. He loved the color yellow and, of course, all kinds of plants and flowers. Hopefully, he's with the love of his life now. He spoke fondly of the woman he adored who'd passed away a few years ago. I think her name was Margie and he truly missed her." He spoke with admiration and regret.

"I wish I had the chance to get to know the real Gus," I said sincerely.

"You would've liked him—the Gus that I finally got to know," Cade replied.

We hugged each other and Cade kissed me deeply. I moaned in response and snuggled into his warmth—I didn't ever want to let go of this incredible man.

"Hannah…you have to stop snuggling against me, baby."

"Oops—sorry about that," I grinned coyly in embarrassment and backed away.

He chuckled and kissed my cheek. The doorbell rang and I clapped my hands with excitement. "Our babies are home!" I couldn't wait to see Boone, Milo, and Jig. We both hurried down the stairs to answer the door.

Cade's parents stood on the front steps and grinned from ear to ear. Boone and Milo yipped with excitement and bounded back and forth around our feet. Jig yowled from inside the cat carrier.

"Okay, dude," I said reassuringly. Taking the crate from Frank, I carried Jig to the sofa and let him out. He meowed with disdain, sniffed me, then checked out every corner of the house. When he returned, he nestled into my lap and purred with contentment. "Yes, sweetie, I'm glad you're home too."

We invited Frank and Esther for a late lunch, and they gladly accepted. It was a great meal, and Frank made us laugh hysterically with his jokes and stories of Cade's antics as a child.

Frank said, "I remember when Cade was about fifteen years old, he desperately wanted to play ball with his friends, but he had to finish the lawn mowing. I never saw anyone drive a rider mower that fast around a yard. When he suddenly hit a large pile of dirt from a destructive mole, he flew off the mower and landed in a heap in Esther's rose bushes. He was so scratched up, he looked like he'd been in a fight with ten feral cats." Frank chuckled, and Esther giggled.

"So, has Cade always shown machinery who's boss?" I asked as I poked a teasing finger into Cade's side. He tickled me back and kissed my cheek.

"Pretty much—and we heard the story about the auger, we weren't surprised. That's my boy!" Esther replied proudly.

"I definitely won that fight," Cade commented with a snicker.

"That you did, Cade. If only I'd gotten that on video," I returned, giving Cade a silly grin.

"Yes, indeedy!" Cade replied.

After Cade's parents left, we decided to go for a walk. The dogs jumped for joy, and it was a beautiful afternoon as we strolled through the woods, following the usual path toward Lois' favorite spot by the lake.

We sat on the driftwood and watched the dogs play along the shore. Cade pulled me close and we talked about everything under the sun. After a while, we sat silently, holding hands and enjoying nature's gorgeous scenery.

"Hannah…"

"Hmm?" I answered but continued to stare at the horizon and the sparkling water of the lake.

"Look at me, sweetheart," he said quietly.

I turned and looked into his chocolate-brown eyes, which reflected sincerity and love.

"Hannah…." Cade fidgeted a bit—which wasn't usual for this man, but I waited for him to continue. "I want you to know that ever since you came into my life…it seems like everything has changed. Crap! I don't know how to say this…I've changed. It's like when we first met; I knew you were the one for me—the woman I'd been waiting for to make my life complete. Does this make any sense to you?"

I didn't know how to respond as I wasn't sure what he was trying to tell me. "I think so."

Cade stood up, then went down on one knee. My eyes grew wide. He pulled a small velvet jewelry box from his pocket and opened it for me. I stared at the contents in surprise. Placed inside the container laid an exquisite diamond engagement ring.

"Hannah, I love you dearly. Will you make me the happiest man alive and marry me?"

"Oh, my Lord!" I blurted too loudly. My gaze went back and forth from the ring to his face, not knowing if this was a good idea.

"Cade…I don't…I'm not sure…oh geez!"

"Hannah, I didn't mean to frighten you with my proposal—"

"No! It's not that. Are you sure about this because I have a lousy track record regarding relationships?" I stared at the stunning ring again and back at his expectant gaze. But what I saw in their depths stunned me.

He really does love me! Do I dare trust him and myself with such an important, life-altering decision? I thought I'd loved Trace, but looking back, I most certainly didn't. But I genuinely love this sensational man and he loves me too!

"Sweetheart, you don't have to answer me now. I know you've been through a lot, and I don't blame you if you find it difficult to give your heart to someone else. You've been burned badly in the past. Would you at least think about it?" Cade asked nervously and returned to sit beside me.

"No! I mean, I love you, Cade. I know it's a little sudden, but I just realized I love you too, with my heart and soul. You're the one I want to spend the rest of my life with." I gently embraced his face in my hands and kissed him passionately as tears of joy slipped down my cheeks.

He kissed me back and replied, "Really? You do?"

"Most definitely, my auger-taming he-man!" I chuckled and snorted a little too loudly. He smiled happily as he took the gorgeous ring from the box and placed it on my finger.

"It's stunning, Cade. I love it!" I kissed him again.

"Ahem…" A soft feminine voice interrupted our make-out session.

Turning to look, I squealed with surprise, "Lois! I've missed you!" She moved forward and I introduced her to Cade.

"So, this is Lois. I thought maybe you were a figment of Hannah's imagination," Cade said. "It's a pleasure to meet you."

"Same here," she replied with a warm smile. "May I join the two of you on the seat?"

"Of course," I answered.

Cade moved down, and Lois sat on the other side of me. The dogs danced around her, and she petted each one, ensuring they received her loving attention.

"Hannah, I came to tell you that I'll be leaving," Lois said as she took one of my hands in hers.

"What…when…why?" I stuttered.

"It's time for me to move on. I finished what I came here to do, and now I must leave. But I'd like to tell you a story before I go." Lois stopped speaking for a few moments and gazed out across the lake. The loons' calls echoed across the water from some distance away, and the fragrant summer breeze wafted around us, cooling our bodies from the hot summer sun.

She continued staring out at the water and began her story. "Shortly after I moved to this town, I was plagued by constant, vivid dreams about a certain young woman. This young lady lived a painful life and would require specific help—help which I knew I could provide. This young lady needed a place where she would be safe and a gentleman who could keep her that way. A man who could not only physically save her life but also give her spiritual and emotional stability as well. I also saw this fellow in my dreams and knew what I had to do." Lois turned to face me now, and I stared at her in wonder.

"The woman I dreamt about was you, dear. I had to save you, and the good Lord told me how to carry out His plan. Since I had no family or relatives, I left my home, property, and all my worldly goods to you, Hannah, as well as explicit instructions for your attorney and Kogi. Everything of mine was bequeathed to you, lock, stock, and barrel. You're living in the cottage that I left specifically for you. I even made sure Cade was hired to improve the cottage so you two would meet. The renovations and supplies were to be completed using my exact specifications with you two in mind. I even made sure the attic was bullet-proofed," Lois said as she patted my hands.

"What?" I found this news confusing, and I couldn't believe what she said could be true.

She stared at my perplexed expression and continued. "My full name is Marjorie Lois Montgomery, but the townspeople knew me as Margie."

Lois squeezed my hand, then said, "Hannah, I died three years ago."

I stood up so abruptly that it rocked the driftwood and Cade used his weight to steady it. Lois also came to her feet and took a firm grip on my upper arms.

She said firmly, "It's true, Hannah. You've been speaking with my spirit and God has done all this for you. He brought me into the picture, along with the doctor who referred you to the one man who could help you escape Trace—good old Kogi. The Lord then gave you Cade and Gus— and don't forget Boone and Jig. He brought you everyone you needed into your life. Always remember what God has done for you and how He's

185

always with you. Now that you're safe, Hannah, it's time for me to move on—to join our Lord in Heaven." She backed up a few steps and turned toward the trail into the woods.

"Wait—Lois!" I called her urgently. Cade stood beside me and he looked bewildered and skeptical.

"Archie, it's time for us to go," Lois called out as she walked away.

When she said "Archie," a familiar figure appeared a few feet away at the path's entrance.

"Gus?!" Both Cade and I yelled in astonishment.

"Hi there, my good friends," he replied with a satisfied smile. I'd never seen Gus smile like this before. His grin made him positively handsome.

"Hannah and Cade, this was and is the love of my life, Angus Archibald Buchanan—whom I called Archie and whom you knew as Gus," Lois said.

"W—what?" I couldn't believe it. It *was* Gus, and Cade looked like he was about to pass out from shock when he saw his good friend back from the dead.

The old man reached out his hand and said, "Margie, it's time for us to go."

Lois took Gus's hand, and before they turned away, their bodies shimmered. We stared in amazement as their appearance went from their current age to somewhere around their early twenties.

"That's so much better," Lois quipped with a giggle. Gus leaned in and kissed her cheek. They strolled down the path and then vanished.

Cade and I sat down hard on the driftwood seat and stared toward the path where they'd disappeared.

"Did that really happen?" Cade asked.

I could only nod in response. We must have sat there for over an hour, contemplating everything Lois told us. *She did all this for me because it was what God wanted.* This knowledge began to sink in, and I couldn't contain myself. I sobbed with overwhelming emotion.

"It's okay, sweetheart. It was their time—and then some," he held me close as he whispered reassuringly into my ear.

"No, it's not that—well, maybe a little. I can't believe God did this for me. Since childhood, I thought I was a screw-up and wasn't worthy of anyone loving me. *You* actually love me and I find out that God's been helping me all along. The man upstairs does exist, and it amazes me how He works through so many people here on this earth. I feel positively blessed. Thank you, Lord." I spoke gratefully toward the heavens. "Thank you, Cade," I turned and kissed him gently. "I love you."

"I love you too, Hannah."

Epilogue

A few months later, Cade and I were in the yard throwing tennis balls for the dogs while sitting on the swing Cade had recently installed. We gazed at the gorgeous plants and flowers that Gus and Huey planted before the nightmare in my attic. Everything was in full bloom with so many vibrant and vivid hues. Gus did a stunning job creating the garden, and I found it a sweet tribute to the old man I'd grown to love.

Phoenix advised us that every crooked person in Trace's organization had been arrested and was awaiting trial. This included the corrupt judge, the D.A., and several police officers. They also discovered that Trace found me at Storm Harbor through my publishing agent. I had no idea Trace knew about her, as I tried to be careful about deleting her emails. That man had been ruthless and conniving and had the memory of an elephant.

The funeral for Gus had been mournful yet sweet. Everyone from the town showed up, and many told funny, sad, and emotional stories about their relationships with the old man. Gus was cantankerous, but after hearing these tales from the townspeople, we discovered he had a big and generous heart. Apparently, he'd helped many people anonymously—but after careful investigation, they knew it was Gus.

Cade was stoic at the funeral, although I knew he took Gus's death hard. But when we met with the old man's attorney, Cade broke down when he discovered Gus left him his mint-condition 1963 Chevy truck. Cade's tears broke my heart. I held him, and we cried together at the loss of the mean, ornery, sweet, kind, generous human being. Since Gus had no immediate family, he left the remainder of his small estate to the local soup kitchen.

Returning my mind to the present, I kissed Cade's cheek.

He turned to me and said, "It's a lovely fall day, my gorgeous bride. What do you say we go for a walk? I know the dogs would love it too." Cade began a trail of gentle kisses down my neck.

"That sounds like a great idea." I giggled when he tickled me in the ribs. "We have enough time before everyone shows up for the barbecue tonight. I can't wait to see your family, Huey, Gator, Wilson, Sheriff Mac, and even 'what can I do ya for' Stanley."

He chuckled and said, "We better get moving, as we have a lot of prep work to do before they get here. Shall we?"

Cade grasped my hand and the dogs followed us out of the gate. As we passed the barn, two horses nickered and trotted over to greet us at the fence. Petting their soft noses, they nuzzled our hands, and we greeted them warmly.

After a few weeks of visiting the stables for my PTSD therapy, I grew to love these large animals. Cade and I found the perfect Quarter Horse pair for sale. A beautiful bay mare for me and a sorrel gelding for Cade. They were well-trained, calm, and sweet—just what we needed for our farm, and they were an added joy to our menagerie. We were even raising some chickens for eggs. Boone loved chasing the poor things around the property, but when the fun was over, he'd snuggle against them for a quick nap.

I was progressing well in dealing with my PTSD because of the equine therapy, and I also attended group therapy regularly for women of domestic violence. It would take time to help heal my old wounds, but I knew this was a good start.

"Mabel and Booker, how are you on this fine afternoon?" I asked the two equines. They nickered once again, then whirled around and took off across the pasture, kicking up their heels in delight. "I guess that answers my question." Giggling, I grabbed Cade's hand and we headed toward the path.

We walked deeper into the woods and enjoyed the sights and scents of God's beauty. Fall was settling in with a heavy hand, and the ground was covered in colorful dried leaves. The trail opened up to our usual private spot on the lake. Sitting on the driftwood, Cade leaned in and kissed me passionately.

"You handsome devil—I do believe you're giving me the vapors!" I uttered in an exaggerated Southern belle accent and fanned my face with my hand. He chuckled deep within his throat and kissed me again. Pulling me onto his lap, I snuggled close to his warm, hard body.

"Darlin', you've turned me into a pile of quivering jelly," he answered. His southern drawl was terrible, which made me giggle, and I kissed his cleft chin.

"We've only been married for six weeks, Cade, but I have to say, I love you more every day—if that's even possible." I snuggled closer.

He sat back a little to look me in the eyes, and his expression turned serious. "I agree, and I never thought I could be this happy. Even my auto repair business is picking up—it's my dream job. You sold your book too, and it's already receiving rave reviews. We have an awesome home and live within a wonderful community. I would have to say we're truly blessed."

"That we are. God gave me my faith back and brought me a marvelous husband and your supportive, loving family. I may have been through many bad things in my life, but what I have now makes it all worth the difficult journey to get here." Cade kissed me on the forehead and pulled me close once again.

We heard a couple of insistent barks, and Boone stood staring at us from the edge of the wooded path. He yipped again, ran in circles, barked once more, then backed up a few steps. Milo was vocal too, and he pushed his nose against something on the ground behind Boone.

"What?" Cade asked.

I got up and approached Boone. "Oh no! Not again!" I replied with dread. The squirming pile consisted of two baby skunks whose eyes weren't yet open. They had a few minor bloody scratches on them, but other than that, they were relatively healthy—at least to my untrained eye. Boone had brought us two more orphaned animals for us to raise.

"We better make sure there isn't a smelly mom in the picture," Cade replied grimly. "It's weird to find baby skunks this time of year. It's late in the season." He carefully picked them up and cuddled them into his arms.

As we scanned the area, I said as I nodded to the baby skunks, "If God brought them to us, then we're supposed to care for Mud Slide and Grease Butt."

Cade guffawed at the names I'd chosen. I giggled and gently stroked the babies. After searching the area, we found the body of the mother skunk. After burying her and saying a prayer, we strolled arm in arm down the path to return to our cottage—our home.

* * *

UNBEKNOWNST TO US, TWO FIGURES WATCHED US FROM A DISTANCE.

"Well, Marjorie Lois Montgomery, we did a bang-up job with these two —with a lot of help from the Lord above, of course."

"We sure did, Archie. But I had to check on Hannah one last time, and it's now time to go home to the Father."

"Now that's a dinkum good idea, Margie—a most heavenly dinkum good idea."

The End

WAIT. DON'T GO JUST YET. PLEASE GO TO THE NEXT PAGE AND SEE OTHER exciting books by Tamara Maudelle available at Amazon...

Also by Tamara Maudelle

"The Holy Warriors' Commission" Series - Book One

SEALING THE GATE

How would you like to start your life over again—and make the ultimate difference *this* time?

Mara, who has been ill her entire life, suddenly wakes up in a new, healthy, youthful body. But this new life comes at a cost. She and the others who are specifically chosen by God for this fight, must find and destroy a formidable and horrifying enemy. They are given a unique set of skills to aid them in their quest, and their adventures also take them on their own personal journeys where they discover love, sorrow, heartbreak, and forgiveness.

Join Mara and her team as they travel to dangerous locations, encounter assistance from strange and surprising sources, then fight a terrifying and dangerous evil who can ultimately take their souls.

Can she and her team find the courage they need, or will they fail in their commission and pay the ultimate price?

JUST RELEASED

"The Holy Warriors' Commission" Series

Book Two

SCROLL OF SEALS

Mara and her team of God's chosen warriors must find a precious holy artifact hidden inside a one-thousand-year-old cavern while staying mere steps ahead of the demon Xerkamedes' foul-smelling servants, the myrmidons.

To gain the information they need, the team must interrogate and rely on the intel from one of the most heinous criminals they have ever encountered. Then they have to fight myrmidons and overcome personal and physical endeavors, which puts Mara and her team not only at odds with their enemies but also with each other.

Will they find the precious artifact in time, and should they believe the information given by a cold-blooded killer? Will this dangerous mission finally take the life of one of their own, and will they succeed in defeating Xerkamedes?

Afterword

Dear Reader:

If you liked my book, I would be very appreciative if you would leave a review on Amazon.

As an author, good book reviews raises our rankings on their website.

If you would like to contact me, you can reach me at tamaramaudelle@ outlook.com.

Thank you!

www.ingramcontent.com/pod-product-compliance
Lightning Source LLC
Chambersburg PA
CBHW020955180626
46814CB00003B/1110